O'BRIEN panda cubs

PANDA CUBS SERIES
where reading begins

O'BRIEN SERIES FOR YOUNG READERS

 panda cubs

O'BRIEN pandas

O'BRIEN panda tales

O'BRIEN flyers

Boo and Bear

Words: Enda Wyley

Pictures: Greg Massardier

THE O'BRIEN PRESS
DUBLIN

First published 2003 by The O'Brien Press Ltd,
12 Terenure Road East, Rathgar, Dublin 6, Ireland
Tel: +353 1 4923333; Fax: +353 1 4922777
E-mail: books@obrien.ie
Website: www.obrien.ie
Reprinted 2007.

ISBN: 978-0-86278-806-3

2 3 4 5 6 7 8 9 10

07 08 09 10 11 12

British Library Cataloguing-in-Publication Data
Wyley, Enda
Boo and bear. - (Solo ; 1)
1.Courage - Juvenile fiction 2.Self-confidence - Juvenile fiction 3.Children's stories
I.Title II.Massardier, Greg 823.9'14[J]

The O'Brien Press receives assistance from

Typesetting, layout, editing: The O'Brien Press Ltd
Printing: Leo Paper Products Ltd China

Can YOU spot the
panda cub
hidden in the story?

Boo was called Boo because she was always **afraid**.

When she was one,

1

Boo was afraid
of having baths!

9

When she was two,

2

Boo was afraid
of the dog next door!

When she
was three,

3

Boo was afraid
of noises in the street!

When she was four,

Boo was afraid of

the
dark!

'Scaredy cat!'
said the kitten.

'Scaredy cat!'
said the puppy.

'Chicken!'
said the crows
in the sky.

'Boo-hoo! Scaredy cat!'
said **Boo**'s big brother.

'Go away!' said **Boo**.

She turned up the TV.

Boo was
a very frightened
little girl.

'What are you afraid of?' asked her Mum. **Boo**'s Mum gave her a big, warm hug.

And **Boo** felt safe –
for a little while.

5

When **Boo** was five,
something very special
happened.
She woke up
on a sunny island.

Bear was with her,
nobody else.

There was soft sand
and a blue sea.
There was warm sun
on **Boo**'s face.
'Look, **Bear**',
said **Boo**.

'Our
very own
island!'

Boo and **Bear**
ran down to the water.
They splashed
in the waves.

28

They made

a huge sandcastle.
Boo made **Bear**

King of the Castle.

Then they were hungry.
Boo found a big tree
and shook it very hard.

Soft, juicy fruit
fell to the ground.

'Yum!' said Boo.

She forgot
to be afraid.

Monkeys came to play.
They swung
Boo and **Bear**
on their special swing.

They went very fast
and very high.

And Boo was
not afraid.

A huge bird took
Boo and **Bear**
to the top of
the highest mountain.

'Look down at the beach!'
said Bear.
Boo was not afraid.

35

When it got dark,
Bear lit a fire.

36

The monkeys
and birds and
Boo and **Bear**
sang songs.

The kittens jumped off
Boo's pyjamas
to keep her warm.

The stars shone
in the sky.

And Boo was
not afraid.

It was time to go home.

The monkeys swung away.

The birds flew up
into the sky.

The fruits went
back on the trees.

The kittens
jumped back onto
Boo's pyjamas.

Next morning,
Boo was home again.

Bear was in her bed.

'Boo-hoo! Scaredy cat!'
said her big brother.

'Scaredy cat!'
said the kitten.

'Scaredy
cat!' said
the puppy.

But **Boo** was
not scared.
She hugged **Bear**.

'I'm not afraid,'
said **Boo**.

And she wasn't.

I HATE EVERYTHING ABOUT YOU!

'Hello, and welcome to another episode of *Where Are They Now?* with me, handsome and award-winning broadcaster, Charlie James. TONIGHT'—there was the sudden sound of dramatic drums and serious trumpets as the theme tune kicked in—'...I talk to the biggest, arguably most controversial band in the history of music. They granted me exclusive access to their comeback gig. It's a story of success, fame, and friendship. How they went from nobodies to the most famous musical act in the world. And how it all came crashing down on that fateful night at the National Talent Gala. What became of the band? Where are they now? Viewers should be aware that some scenes may feature bright flashing images, mostly when I flash my perfect and very white teeth. I'm sorry, but there's nothing I can do about that,' said Charlie, flashing a bright white grin. 'NOW, LET'S GOOOOOOO!'

The rest of the theme tuned played; there were lots of dramatic shots of Charlie James running after people with his camera, like he was a journalistic superhero tracking down celebrities of years gone past. As the show played out across the country, the streets seemed a little quieter across Britain. Maybe it was a coincidence, or maybe it's because everyone had snuck home early to find out the next chapter of this extraordinary story: how two friends became the biggest, brightest stars in the world, and how they lost it all.

'So guys, I wonder if you could tell us how it all began for you. Was music always a big part of your life?' Charlie asked, holding out a microphone in front of two twelve-year-old boys. Ollie was swigging from a fizzy pop bottle as he sat with a huge mirror behind him, surrounded by flowers and cards from well-wishers. Sat next to him surrounded by every type of fruit imaginable was his best friend, Hector.

'Well Charlie, music was definitely where it started. We always loved music, and we had a feeling it was our ticket to the big time. You may have called us dreamers.' Ollie smiled. 'I guess that this gig is about, you know, getting back together after all that was said and done, trying to write the perfect ending to a crazy dream.'

'That's absolutely right, Ollie. It always felt like we had unfinished business,' Hector agreed.

'And have you two made up? I know that things haven't always been easy,' Charlie asked.

'Yeah . . .' Ollie and Hector both replied.

'We're all good,' Ollie said, taking over the conversation. 'For me this has always been about other people—that connection—whether that's with strangers or friends. There is no 'I' in music after all, Charlie.'

'Well yeah, there is,' Hector replied.

'Well, obviously there is an 'i' in it. What I mean is that I like to think of it as a gift for others, like a really good gift, you know? Not like a book token or some bubble bath, but a really good one, like a dolphin. I like to think about the dolphins when I make music; I just really want to save the dolphins I guess.'

'Is there a shortage of dolphins?' Hector asked.

'Can you have too many dolphins?' Ollie replied.

'Yes, too many dolphins would be a nightmare. Imagine if you were trying to walk down the street but you had to keep stepping over dolphins all the time.'

4

'What about you, Hector? Do you make music for the animals?' Charlie asked, a tad confused.

'I make music for the fans,' Hector replied. 'They're the ones who buy, or rather bought our music. I mean, I don't think a dolphin has ever bought any of our stuff?'

'Are you making fun of me?' Ollie asked. 'Do you not care about the elephants and the dolphins?'

'Elephants now, is it? Yes, I care about all the animals, but I just care about the fans more,' Hector snapped.

'So anyway,' Charlie tried to interrupt.

'Are you saying I don't care about the fans?' Ollie asked indignantly.

'I'm not saying anything,' Hector shrugged.

'Oh, you seem to be saying quite a lot! This is typical of you isn't it, all sighing and silences. Don't think I haven't noticed them. You better watch it . . .'

'Watch what? What are you going to do?'

'I can do what I like, this is my band; one phone call and you're gone forever!' screamed Ollie.

'Gone? What do you mean gone? Are you

threatening to do away with me, you know, kill me?!
You heard that guys didn't you?' Hector said, talking to
the camera crew. 'He wants me dead! Call the police!
No, call my publicists!'

'No, not kill you!' Ollie yelled. 'I mean fire you!'

'Fire me?! That's worse!' screeched Hector.

'How is it worse than killing you?'

'Because it is! How are *you* going to fire *me*?'

'By firing you, that's how I'm going to fire you!'
Ollie stood up. This was quickly escalating into a
blazing row.

The camera operator looked at Charlie James, who
mouthed 'keep rolling' back at him. Charlie knew this
was gold. A blazing row would be great TV viewing.

'FIRE ME!? You can't fire me; it's not *your* band!'
Hector said, getting to his feet. 'Maybe I'll fire *you*!' he
said, prodding a finger into Ollie's shoulder.

'Did you just . . . just . . . prod me?!' Ollie said,
looking in horror at Hector's finger. 'You know I have
issues with my personal space. You need spiritual
permission to come into my personal space!'

'Spiritual permission?! You've lost it mate. You're

lost in showbiz!'

'Me!' Ollie replied in horror. 'You can talk. I mean, you have to have a basket of fruit with you wherever you go! That's not normal!'

'Oh, here you go again, always with the fruit mockery.'

'Keep this up and you'll be off, out on your ear,' Ollie threatened.

'I told you, you can't do that; it's my band too!' Hector screamed back.

'NO, IT'S MINE!' Ollie bellowed.

'IT'S MY KEYBOARD!'

'IT'S MY RECORDING EQUIPMENT!'

'MY LYRICS!'

'My . . . CAT!' Ollie yelled at the top of his voice.

'What, oh you really want to go there, do you?' Hector snapped.

'Boys! Boys!' Charlie intervened. 'I'm sure your fans don't want to see you arguing like this. But as you mention Nigel, why don't you both, in your own words, tell me how it started?

REACH FOR THE STARS

'Three . . . two . . . one . . . GO!' Hector started, before suddenly becoming self-conscious. 'You know, Ollie, this feels a bit weird, pretending to interview each other for TV. I mean, it's never going to happen is it? We're never going to get that famous!' Hector said. 'Also people are looking at us.' Ollie and Hector looked around; they were getting some very odd looks from strangers on the streets as they trudged to school.

'We might. You've got to think big. What if we become overnight successes and we have to talk about our music to the waiting world? We need to be prepared. We need to be professional. So get back in the zone and point that hairbrush at me like it's a mic,' Ollie said.

'Okay, okay.' Hector shrugged. 'We are live on air with the man of the moment, Ollie, from probably the greatest rock band in the world. Do you mind if we grab a few words with you before the awards ceremony?'

'No, not at all. Anything for the fans. I mean, the fans are what it's all about.'

'Too right, dude. Firstly, congrats on your band being voted the greatest band of all time,' Hector said, doing his best 'interviewer' voice.

'Thanks bro. It's pretty amazing considering that I'm only twelve years old. I know those guys from The Beatles had me on the ropes for a while back there, but I'm just really glad we finally put this whole "who's the greatest?" thing to bed once and for all. But I couldn't have done it without my best friend, Hector. We're like brothers from different parents.'

'Do you mean *bruthas from other muthas*?'

'Morning Nigel,' said Ollie, having a momentary lapse of concentration as he walked past his cat. I say his cat, but no one really owned Nigel; he seemed to have lived in most houses in the area at one time or another. He was like a little furry nomad. 'Where

were we?' said Ollie, switching back to interview mode. 'Oh yes, that's it, we're bruthas from other muthas . . . that.'

'Hector couldn't be here for tonight's award ceremony could he?'

'No, he's—'

'Collecting FIFA World Player of the Year, I understand?' said Hector, with a gleeful look on his face.

'What? Yes of course. He's er . . . very talented,' Ollie said, narrowing his eyes.

'Yes, I heard that too. Isn't this the first time that any member of a band has also been voted the greatest footballer of all time as well?'

'Er, yes, it's almost unbelievable isn't it?' Ollie said sarcastically, as they crossed the road opposite the school gates.

'Well, good luck for tonight, even though you've already won. I mean it's really nice that the people in charge of the Oscars, the Grammys, and the Nobel Peace Prize got together to make this super award; it's really kind of them. Oh, before we finish you must tell me what it was like to be the first rock star on Mars!'

'Right, this is silly—FIFA player of the year as well as a mission to Mars? This wouldn't happen. Will you take this seriously, please?' Ollie snapped.

'It might happen!' Hector huffed, throwing his arms into the air. 'You don't know that we *won't* get that award, and I *might* get FIFA footballer of the year,' Hector said as they approached the school gates.

'Oi, what are you two doing with that hairbrush?' a boy with a thick pair of eyebrows asked.

'Er, nothing,' Hector said putting it back in his bag. The two had been so engrossed that they hadn't noticed they were practically in school by the time the interview had finished.

'What flavour crisps have you got today?' the boy asked.

'Cheese and onion I think, Bill.'

'I don't like those,' Bill huffed. 'Can you get some

different ones?'

'Well, maybe don't keep stealing mine? Maybe, buy your own?' Ollie sighed.

'No, I don't want to. I'll have the cheese and onion, if that's the only choice.' Bill rolled his eyes dramatically.

'That's very understanding of you, Bill. Do you want them now or shall I give them to you later?'

'Later, or they'll get all crunched up,' Bill said, before scuttling away.

'What sort of world do we live in where I get robbed, but only at a convenient time to my assailant?' Ollie grumbled.

'What does assailant mean?' Hector asked.

'It means criminal. I saw it on CSI Miami last night,' Ollie replied. 'Anyway, where was I? Oh yes, how can you become FIFA Player of the Year when you can't even play football? We both know it makes your cheeks sweat too much.'

'I play a lot of FIFA on the PlayStation, and that's practically the same as the real thing.' Hector shrugged. 'Stop killing my buzz.'

'Look, if we're going to do the pretend interview stuff, I just think we should keep it realistic, you know. Stick to us being the greatest band in the world, and lose the space bit and the footballing stuff. But for a first interview that was okay, and practice makes perfect—isn't that the key to being a rock star?'

'Yeah.' Hector grinned.

'Although I think when they talk about practice making perfect, they probably mean practising playing musical instruments.'

'Listen Ollie, we could sit around playing and practising music, learning to play, actually writing a proper song, but what would that actually get us?' Hector asked.

'Better?' Ollie said hopefully.

'It all sounds a bit serious to me. Anyway, rock and roll isn't *just* about the music; it's about the whole package. We did write this all down,' Hector said holding up a tatty piece of A4 paper. On it was scrawled 'The Manifesto for World Domination: a to-do list that every aspiring rock and roll band needs.'

The Manifesto for WORLD DOMINATION

Number one was a distinctive band name. It was the most important of the things on there, one that needed the greatest thought put into it, and because it was so important, it remained blank.

Number two was looking good.

Three was talking cool.

Four was a striking hairstyle.

Five was deciding how they were going to spend all the many millions that the band would make.

And lastly, was the actual song. The trouble was that Ollie and Hector were still undecided about their sound too and therefore hadn't actually bothered to pick up an instrument and play anything yet. Hard to believe I know, but this was probably the only band in the history of the world that had never played a note together.

'It would be nice, wouldn't it, if we were in a proper rock band? Then we'd be cool and people might like us at school a bit more. Imagine that, people actually liking us. I mean if we want to climb the social ladder of popularity then we have to do something cool, something that we will be remembered for. Like being the best rock band in the world.' Ollie's eyes glazed over as he imagined his name in lights and what it would be like to have the entire school want to be his friend. He might get to go to all the parties. He might not get his crisps stolen every lunchtime.

'I think it'll just be a good laugh!' Hector smiled. Hector had all the same problems as Ollie, but he didn't seem to care the way Ollie did. Ollie tried to follow Hector's lead, but he just couldn't cope in the same way that Hector could. Yes, people stole stuff off Hector too, but he would simply get on with school life, and as much as Ollie tried to copy his friend he just couldn't do it.

Ollie and Hector wandered in through the school gates. There was the usual throng of yelling and chasing and footballs flying in a million directions at what looked like a million miles an hour. 'I've been thinking about our name,' Hector said, pulling out a piece of paper as they headed to their form rooms. 'Okay, what about these . . . Badly Folded Dreams?'

'Er . . . '

'Ping Pong Waddle Ding Bat?'

'Hmm.'

'The Snogs? Jimmy and the Plastic Paper People? Abraham Meatcake? The Spits? Geriatric Gnome Circus? The Rolling Stones?'

'Don't they already exist?'

'Yes, but our version would be spelled with seventeen Rs.'

'Hmm.'

'Okay, okay, what about The Fire Extinguishers?'

'No.'

'The Desk?'

'Not good.'

'Wallpaper Shelf . . . Unit . . . ?'

'Are you just naming stuff you can see?'

'Yeah, kind of.'

'We'll come back to the name,' Ollie said, stopping outside Hector's classroom. 'I wish we could just get on with being rock stars. It feels like we've done all this work and no one knows about us. Why can't we just get a mega-huge record deal and release our masterpiece into the world?'

'Well, I think we have to actually send our music to someone so they can hear it.'

'Are we even ready for the world to hear it? Where do you even find record executives?'

'Wait . . .' Hector said. 'We don't. They find us!'

'Eh?'

'I've got an idea. A big beautiful idea!' Hector beamed.

BRRRRRRRING! The bell began to ring for the start of lessons.

'Meet me here at the end of the day,' Hector giggled. 'This plan is so brilliant you could give it a tickle!'

TWISTED SISTER

'So, what's the idea?' Ollie asked, catching up with Hector in the busy school corridor.

'Well,' Hector said, grinning, 'here's the plan—'

'What are you pair of snowflakes up to?' interrupted the steely voice of Hannah, Ollie's tormentor-in-chief, all round mocker, and big sister.

'Er . . . hi!' Hector smiled. Hector had a bit of a crush on Hannah which he confessed to Ollie one sleepover after a late-night binge session of KitKats and Cherry Fanta. Ollie decided that it was weird and made him feel strange inside. The two of them agreed then and there never to talk about it ever again.

'Nothing, you know, we're just, you know, I mean . . . we erm . . . what was the question?' replied Ollie.

'Well covered up, man,' Hector whispered in his ear.

'You're definitely up to something,' Hannah said, narrowing her eyes. 'I can tell, and I don't like not knowing what I don't know,' Hannah said cryptically. 'Whatever it is, stay out of my bedroom, my way, and my life forever—got it?'

'Hey, Hannah.' A tall Year 10 boy nodded in their direction as he made his way down the corridor.

'Oh hey, Darren.' Hannah grinned, before going a little pink.

'Who's that?' Hector said, looking concerned.

'Darren Ledbetter,' Hannah said slightly gooerly.

'Are you okay?' Ollie asked. 'You've gone a very strange shade of pink. Do you have a crush on that Darren Ledbetter boy?'

'Who has a crush on Darren Ledbetter?' one boy asked, totally butting into their conversation.

'Not me!' Hannah protested as she shot Ollie a burning look that he felt singe his face.

'I definitely didn't say that she had a crush on Darren Ledbetter!' Ollie backtracked.

'JUST SHUUUUT UP ABOUT DARREN LEDBETTER, OLLIE!' Hannah cried.

'You have a crush on Darren Ledbetter?' another girl asked. It was one of Hannah's friends. 'I knew it! Hey, it's true, Hannah *does* have a crush on Darren,' the girl announced to a crowded corridor. There was the usual whooping and yelling as the gossip made its way around the school.

'You will pay for this. Probably with your life,' Hannah whispered gruffly, her face now fully flushed with embarrassment, before she skulked off to try and undo Ollie's mess.

'Well that's just perfect. Oh boy . . .' Ollie said panting with panic.

'Are you scared of your sister?' Hector leaned in and asked.

'What a stupid question! Of course I am. I shouldn't have mentioned Darren; it sort of popped out. I was meddling with dark forces by saying that. Do you not remember what Hannah's capable of? Every good idea that we've ever had she's been responsible for destroying, breaking, crushing and all the other words that end in 'ing'. Bad words! Do you remember the time we invented a new sport, UFC?'

'Ultimate Fighting Chess? Yes, it was a classic!' Hector agreed.

'Who was it that karate-chopped the board in half and tried to insert that tiny horse piece inside me? Hannah.'

'Oh yes, I do remember that.'

'Or the time that we tried to invent a new colour; we thought it would be the answer to becoming famous and getting rich?' Ollie asked.

'Oh, yes. Who knew that literally all the colours

23

were already invented?' Hector shrugged.

'Who emptied a tin of orange paint on our heads, forcefully, from quite a big height?'

'Hannah,' they both said.

'Mind you, she is quite attractive when she's feisty . . .' Hector mused.

'We're not talking about any of that are we?' Ollie said, trying to remind Hector of their pledge. 'Let's change the subject—you were going to tell me your idea.'

'Walk and talk, boss, walk and talk,' Hector said, leading the way out of the school. 'Well, what do we spend all our days doing?'

'Band stuff?' Ollie said.

'Such as?'

'Well, pretend interviews, deciding on our sound by looking at old videos and stuff. You know, research. In order to be a band, you have to think like a band!' Ollie said, like a soldier repeating orders.

'Specifically?' Hector asked encouragingly.

'Well, on YouTube mostly, seeing what's out

there, seeing what we need to do to take over the world.'

'Exactly!'

'Exactly what?'

'Why don't we just put our music on there? We don't need to wait for the phone to ring. Let's put ourselves out there, let the world see our greatness!' Hector grinned.

'You mean, just release a song ourselves?' Ollie said, mulling over the idea.

'Think of it as setting our music free! If it takes off, great; if it doesn't, and no one notices, then so what? No harm done.'

'But are we ready?'

'What are we waiting for?' Hector said.

'Well . . . we don't have a song?' Ollie clarified.

That's right. Ollie and Hector had spent so much time thinking of the name, working out what sort of band they might be, and deciding what to wear, that neither of them had bothered to write a song. All they'd ever done was plug in their instruments and admired how cool they looked in the big mirror in

Ollie's Mum's bedroom.

'Let's do it now!' Hector enthused. 'I mean, look, how long can it possibly take to write a five-minute song? Must be half an hour—tops.'

'But what about our sound? What's our sound going to be? WE NEED A SOUND, HECTOR!!!!' Ollie said, panic erupting from his voice.

'Relax, I know our sound; it came to me like a flash during geography. The teacher was talking about glaciers or something, and then it landed in my brain like a brick,' Hector said, smiling. 'All the things that we've been talking about: a sound that's going to change the world, something that you can dance to, something that you can rock out to, one word that describes all those things . . . it's *COOL!*'

'Well, it is hard to argue with that logic,' Ollie said grinning. He took a deep breath. 'Okay, let's do it!' He beamed. 'Half an hour?'

'At the most!' Hector grinned back. 'I say we write it, record it, upload it, and by this time next week, be world famous? Sound like a plan?'

Hector was right; what were they waiting for?

All this band talk was just talk, but now they had nothing to stop them. 'It's going to be brilliant. We've got nothing to lose! I'll get some snacks, you bring the stuff over!'

4

PUMP UP THE JAM

Ollie had only been home for about five minutes when he heard the usual thudding of footsteps to indicate that Hector was here too. But it was just enough time for Ollie to lay out some snacks. If you wanted to get anything out of Hector, you had to feed him. It was a smorgasbord of beige: Hector hated anything that was either a fruit or vegetable. There were sausage rolls, Pringles, some sort of egg wrapped in more sausage, or was it a sausage wrapped in egg? And some sliced white bread to put it all in. Along with some pretend Coca-Cola that Ollie's mum bought in bulk from the German supermarket.

'Where is he, the musical genius and soon-to-be millionaire?' Hector said, popping his head round Ollie's bedroom door. 'Ooo, hello Nigel,' Hector said, passing Ollie's cat as it stalked down the hall giving Hector a threatening hiss. 'Always so angry, Nige.'

Hector was dressed in sunglasses, his hoodie with a sausage dog on the front, and trainers that he'd covered in glitter. It was the rock star look . . . of sorts.

'Make way for the superstar!' Are the pillows plump enough for you, sir?' Hector teased, as if Ollie was the most famous boy in the world. 'No paparazzi!' Hector yelled out down the hall. 'I'm only kidding . . . there's no one there. Come on, let's crack open the Kooka-Koola and get ready for world domination.'

'Are you sure this is going to work?' Ollie asked.

'I've no idea, but it's exciting isn't it?!' Hector grinned.

Ollie grabbed the guitar and plugged it into the keyboard before handing it to Hector who began to twang and strum. 'Do you ever think it's weird that the people who made our keyboard—'

'Yamaha?' Ollie said.

'Yep, Yamaha, also make motorbikes and tennis rackets?'

'That is weird. It'd be like if Fiat started making cricket bats and bassoons,' Ollie theorized as he plugged a mic into the keyboard and then the keyboard into his laptop.

'I've been working on a rap.' Hector grinned.

'Rap? I didn't know you could rap.'

'Neither did I!' said Hector. 'Although I'm a bit stuck; all I've got so far is: Yo peeps, can't you see, I'm the coolest MC since . . .' Hector paused trying to think of his next line.

'Cheddar cheese?' Ollie suggested.

'I don't think it screams cool . . .' Hector replied.

'Hmm . . . I'm the coolest MC since . . . Humpty DumpteeeEEEE?'

'Mediterranean seeeeea . . . The *Ten o'clock News* on the BBCccccCCCCCCC . . .' Hector tried out. Ollie and Hector looked at each other. 'Maybe we could leave the rap bit out?' suggested Hector.

'Yeah, save it for the second single,' Ollie said, nodding.

'Sounds good to me. Why don't we make the first song about love and stuff? People are always singing about that.'

'You're right, they are. Okay, let's call it *Baby, I Love You Baby*.'

'That is perfect!' Hector grinned. 'Let's get recording!'

★

'This may be the best thing I've ever heard. A band, huh? This will be perfect. They've come up with their own revenge.' Hannah grinned from the dark landing outside of Ollie's bedroom. 'Now, how best to make this a recording session they'll never forget,' she said, stroking Nigel under his chin.

★

'Musical instruments all plugged in?' Hector asked. 'And are we ready to record on your laptop?'

'Check and check!' Ollie beamed.

'Right, take it away!' Hector cried out.

'WAIT!' Ollie shouted. 'I don't know what to

play. Or really how to play.'

Hector looked at his watch. I need to be home by eight, it's all kicking-off on Emmerdale this week; we don't have time to learn. Let's just jam, press record, and see where the vibe goes?'

'One . . . two . . . three . . . four!' Ollie cried, hitting the big red button on the keyboard. A mechanical drumbeat started to play. Hector looked around, grabbed a recorder, and blew into it.

'Whoa, yeah, that's got some soul!' Ollie said, nodding his head back and forth, totally lost in the music. 'Hector, what do you call that?'

'It's called a scale,' Hector replied. 'That's what they taught us in recorder class, before I was thrown out.'

'Kicked out? That's very rock 'n' roll. Why, were you too dangerous for them?'

'No, I just didn't bother to learn anything else and basically just mimed when it came to concerts,' Hector said, sounding embarrassed.

'Well, it's great! I love those notes you just

played. What were they?' Ollie said enthusiastically as Hector blew into a recorder while twanging his electric guitar.

'C, D, and a . . . wait is it an H? How far do the letters go up?'

'G, I think,' replied Ollie.

'Okay, it's probably not an H in that case. I wonder if I can . . . yes, I can play the guitar with the recorder!' Hector said excitedly.

'Great, now if I add a samba beat,' Ollie said, hitting a button on the keyboard. 'Ooooooooooh, that's funky. I know this is only our first attempt at recording ourselves, and we don't know what we're really doing, but this has "hit" written all over it,' Ollie said, bobbing around like he was listening to the best song he'd ever heard in his life. 'What do we do about lyrics? I don't think we should rap again. We could just say some cool words; that's much better than a rap, because it doesn't have to rhyme.'

'Perfect! I'll start, then you can join in!' Hector said, giving Ollie a thumbs-up. 'Ahem . . . Baby . . .'

'Yes darling?' Ollie replied.

'No, I'm singing now. This is me singing.'

'Oh sorry—go for it,' Ollie said, nodding along to the samba beat.

'Baaaaaaby, I love you baby!!!!!!' Hector cried out. 'Wave your hands in the air like you just don't care.' At which point, Ollie did. 'No, not you, you need to keep playing.'

'Oops,' Ollie said, going back to playing the keys.

What happened over the next few minutes is hard to explain. Words were said, or rather sung. whether that officially makes them a song or not is hard to say. Here's a rough transcript:

'Two times! I mean twice.'

'Baaaaby, I love you baby!'

'Ooooooh.' (About thirty times.)

'Yeah.'

'Drop it like it's hot.'

'Can I get a whoop-whoop?'

'Yes you can-whoop-whoop.'

'Thanks for the whoop-whoop.'

'Oh, you're welcome. Any time, mate.'

Ollie winked at Hector. By now they were both so completely and utterly absorbed by their own greatness that the world outside became completely irrelevant. Nothing was going to interrupt their electric jazz slam. They sang, and danced, and hit things that made noises, all the noises, while they had their eyes closed, the way that rock stars do on TV. But perhaps it would have been better if they had kept their eyes open; they might have seen what was about to enter the room, or should I say who.

OK COMPUTER

For most cats, music is irrelevant to them. They don't tend to dance, sing or join in, in any way. Maybe it was Ollie and Hector's music that got under Nigel's skin, or perhaps it was the fact that he wasn't like most cats. But something about the sights and sounds of Ollie and Hector, performing what looked to Nigel like some sort of tribal ritual, sent him into a bit of a spin, and Nigel went rogue. He started running around the room in circles like his tail was on fire, over the bed, along the shelf, and then landed on the keyboard.

'CLANG CLING PLINK PLONK!' the keyboard yelped like it was in pain, as Nigel ran from one end to the other before starting the whole merry-go-round again.

'Nooooooo!' Ollie yelled out.

'Cat attack!' Hector cried.

'Someone fetch the mum!' Ollie said in a panic, his words getting slightly stuck as he tried to spit them out.

'Yooooooooooow!' Hector yelled, trying to reach Nigel as he zoomed past for what was his seventh circuit of the room. They could hear Ollie's mum shouting, 'KEEP THAT NOISE DOWN!' so loudly that the mic was bound to have picked it up.

'The sound's too loud—drop the beat!' Ollie yelled to Hector.

'I can't!' he bellowed, trying to figure out how the keyboard worked.

'Go, go, GOOOOO!' Ollie yelled, grabbing an idle ukulele and waving it around like a giant fly swat. The cat finally took the hint and landed on the keyboard of the computer.

'What! No, Nigel!' Ollie cried out as Nigel appeared to tap dance away on the keys.

'He's doing something to our recording!' Ollie yelled out, trying to grab him. The sounds that Ollie and Hector had been recording from the keyboard through the computer were suddenly being shaken around. Their lyrics were being slowed down and repeated. The cat was inadvertently remixing Ollie and Hector's musical masterpiece.

'How's he doing that?' Hector said, trying to shoo Nigel away.

'I don't know!'

'What *is* all that noise?!' Mum screamed, bounding up the stairs. 'I am trying to have five minutes peace and a cup of tea down here!'

'Sorry, it was Nigel,' Ollie explained, finally yanking the recording cable out of the laptop and hitting the off button on his Yamaha, bringing the thumping rhythm of the electronic beats to an end.

'No, you can't blame all that on the cat. Cats can't play the guitar,' Mum said sternly.

'Well, yes, some of it was us. We're sort of in a band,' Ollie said, picking up Nigel.

'Yeah, I kind of gathered,' Dad said, coming

to the doorway. 'It sounds like the end of days,' he blustered. 'I could hear it from the shed!'

'Come on Nigel, time for you to go!' Ollie said.

'He's ruined our song; we can't upload that!' Hector sighed as he held the door open for Ollie. 'We'll have to go again, there's no time to lose . . . oh, do I smell dinner?'

Hector and Ollie followed the scent of dinner downstairs, and for a few seconds Ollie's bedroom was quiet and empty again; the noise and chaos had disappeared. That is, until the sound of laughing rang through the air. 'Hahaha!' Hannah gasped with breathless laughter as she burst through the door of Ollie's bedroom. Her face was glistening with tears, her stomach aching with laughter. This was the greatest day of her life, no two ways about it. Thanks to Nigel, her plan had just got ten times better. She had the worst music in history; now all she needed was to give it to the world. Thirty seconds at Ollie's computer and her trophy for World's Most Annoying Big Sister was in the bag! She would have her revenge.

'Well, you wanted to be stars, now's your chance

boys,' she giggled. All she needed was a picture to
go with the sound. 'It's a shame that the webcam
wasn't on to record the whole thing, but you can't
have everything. Let's find a nice picture of the two
of you,' Hannah said, searching through Ollie's files
on his laptop. Here we are—a nice one of the pair of
you dressed as Batman and Robin. Perfect! You both
look ridiculous. Now, a good name. Oh yes, how
about The Twerpz? Perfect for a right pair of twerps.
And, what shall we call the song . . . hmmm . . . *Cat
Attack* seems appropriate,' Hannah said, typing away
on Ollie's laptop.

'Your mum could have told us that dinner wasn't
actually ready before we made it all the way
downstairs,' said Hector, entering Ollie's bedroom.

'To be fair, Hector, she tried to say something,
but you barged past her and ran down the stairs
before you could be stopped,' replied Ollie.

'Hey, what's happening?' Hector said, clocking
Hannah at the laptop.

'What are you doing in here, Hannah? You're

not uploading our music!?' Ollie said in horror, as he spotted the upload page with his and Hector's photo on it. 'That wasn't our music. Nigel made that. It sounded awful. Are you insane?!'

Ollie lunged towards the laptop, to try and grab her hand away from the button.

'Hey HEY HEEEEY! NO ONE MOVE!' Hannah yelled, her finger hovering dangerously above the return key on the keyboard. Ollie slowly backed away.

'She's bluffing!' Hector said, looking over at Ollie.

'Do you really want to risk it?' Hannah said, her finger twitching with anticipation. It was like cowboys at high noon.

'Seriously Hannah, do not upload that video. We'll be a laughing stock to the entire world,' Ollie pleaded.

'If you're trying to dissuade me, you're going the wrong way about it,' she said, grinning.

'Is this about Darren Ledbetter?' Ollie asked.

'SHUT UP ABOUT DARREN LEDBETTER!' shouted Hannah, suddenly enraged. 'BECAUSE OF YOU I'M THE LAUGHING STOCK OF THE ENTIRE SCHOOL.'

'I'm sure everyone will have forgotten about it in a month or two,' Ollie said, in an attempt to defuse the situation.

'A MONTH OR TWO?! THAT'S IT! I'M DOING IT! I DON'T CARE!' and with that Hannah hit upload. Ollie dived across the room and made a grab for the laptop, trying to knock Hannah out of the way. They each had a firm grip on either side of the computer, locked in a tug of war.

That is, until Hannah smirked, and let go, sending Ollie and the laptop flying across the room.

'Hannah!' Hector yelled out. 'Why would you do that?! I mean, I will forgive you, but you're going to have to make this right. I'm thinking dinner, somewhere fancy. Tell me, do you like kebabs?'

'Hector!' Ollie cried out. 'Not the time!'

'It's okay, it's okay,' Hector cried out. 'Let's just delete the video. We can take it down before anyone sees it.'

'You're right. Of course!' Ollie scrambled across

the floor to the laptop. 'Please don't be broken, please don't be broken. Ah ha!' he said triumphantly, as the laptop started up perfectly. Now, I just need to head to YouTube and delete the video, here we are . . . enter your password. . .' Ollie said out loud.

'Okay, so put in the password and let's take this bad boy down.' Hector grinned smugly. 'Are you still on for kebabs, Hannah?'

'Not a chance,' Hannah replied.

'Enter password . . .' Ollie said again blankly, looking at Hector. The YouTube account was set up some years ago, as a way of making Minecraft videos to share with friends, but it was never used; it had just sort of sat there.

'Oh no, you don't know the password. You must remember, you must!' Hector said, realizing what was going on.

'Er . . .'

At this point, Hannah burst into uncontrollable laughter.

'The password!' Hector cried. 'Is it your date of birth, your age, your favourite football team? Has it got a seven in it or thirty-four? Think!'

'Stop saying numbers at me; it was a long time ago!' said Ollie, flustered.

'Well, just try all of those in all of the combinations,' Hector suggested.

'All the combinations of all the numbers that I know? You want me to do that?' Ollie snapped. 'Let's see what we're dealing with here,' Ollie said, clicking onto the video. The screen showed a blurry picture of Ollie and Hector, in superhero costumes with the description: First single from the greatest band in the world—The Twerpz. Music thumped from the laptop speakers, occasionally stopping and reversing, all the while random lyrics spewed out: 'Oh baby, fetch the mum! What *is* all that noise?! CAT ATTACK!' Imagine the opposite of music; if you can imagine that, then you can imagine how bad it sounded.

'Look, we've had two views! We have two views! Okay, one of those is us, but someone else in the world has also seen it!' Hector cried.

'Hannah, what have you done?!' Ollie said, madly typing every word and number that he could think of into the login screen.

Hannah, who had finally recovered from a fit of laugher replied, 'Me? I was only going to upload it for half an hour, then take it down again. It's not my fault you've forgotten your password. I mean who forgets their password? That's like the one thing you're not supposed to do.'

'LOCKED OUT! I'M LOCKED OUT OF MY ACCOUNT FOR TWENTY-FOUR HOURS! TOO MANY INCORRECT GUESSES! NOOOOOOOOOOOOO!'

ALL AROUND THE WORLD

'Hello, I'm Charlie James. This is the news at breakfast. The headlines this morning: with the presidential elections around the corner, we'll look at the front runner, Hank Jones. We'll also be talking to a boy who claims to have saved Christmas, but first—who are The Twerpz? It's the question that the whole world seems to be asking. It all started when the mystery band posted a video to social media. In a matter of a few short hours, their song, *Cat Attack*, has become the most watched video on YouTube. On views alone they are number one around the world, with this new style of anti-music music. But, who are The Twerpz, the inventors of this spiky new musical genre some are already calling To-Be-Boogie? We're now joined by Neal Twazz, music journalist and cultural commentator. Neal, thanks for joining us. So firstly, shall we start with the 'who'? Who are The Twerpz? Are they world-famous pop stars hiding behind secret identities?'

'Well, thanks for having me, Charlie. I just want to say that I don't believe the rumours that it's The Beatles, Jay-Z, and Lady Gaga all rolled into one. And I'll tell you why: I simply don't think that these people are capable of coming up with something like the song The Twerpz released. And I don't think it's any exaggeration to say that nothing will ever be the same after this. It's like the moon landing of music; it's the splitting of the atom of sound. It's like they've taken the rules of what actually sounds like music and said: we're not going to follow that, we're doing our own thing. It's almost like they're not musicians at all, just wild beasts of funk. You might hear them and think—these people have no talent whatsoever; they're clearly just making a load of noise, with some words put over the top. Maybe that's the point, who knows? Maybe no one, maybe everyone!'

'In many ways that makes no sense, and yet, it makes complete sense,' replied Charlie. 'Do you think they'll be offered a multi-million pound deal, Neal?'

'Who knows? All I can tell you is that every record label worth their salt will be after this group, if it is indeed a group.'

'Yes, there is already talk of national newspapers offering rewards to track down this gang of music pushers. How they have managed to hide their genius from the world so far is a mystery. Someone, somewhere, knows who they are.'

'Exactly. That's why I'm certain that these people aren't famous pop stars. It's a small world, and I don't think that people would be able to keep it secret.

Only someone or *something* brand new on the scene would be able to come up with something like this.'

'*Something,* Neal?'

'That's right, I'm not ruling out aliens, or robots from the future.'

'Neal Twazz, thank you for sharing your brain with us. For those of you who haven't heard *Cat Attack*, here's a clip of the viral hit . . .'

'*Cat Attack*?' Ollie's mum said, watching the news as she set about frying eggs for breakfast. At that second, the now familiar clip of Nigel on the keyboard and the sound of Ollie, Hector, and Ollie's mum's words being sung forwards, backwards, and sideways floated out from the TV. 'Oh, my gosh! That's me! I've become a virus!!!'

'Morning Mrs T!' Hector said, popping through the back door. 'Something smells delish! Are you okay? You've gone a funny colour. Do you have a virus?'

'Yes, I think I do; the man on the TV said so.'

'When the people on TV start sending you messages, Mrs T, you know it's time to turn it off.'

Ollie's mum ran to the foot of the stairs and screamed, 'HANNAH, OLLIEEEEE! COME DOWN, NOW!'

After a second of silence, Ollie bounded breathlessly down the stairs with Hannah in tow, both rubbing their eyes trying to wake up.

'Hector, why are you here in your school uniform? It's Saturday,' Ollie said, his eyes adjusting to the light.

'Oh no, not again,' groaned Hector.

'What's the matter, Mum?' Hannah asked.

'We're famous!' Ollie's mum shouted.

'What? Are you okay, Mum? You look funny.'

'Famous!' she blurted out again. 'YouTube.
Famous. Man. TV. Aliens,' she spluttered.

'YouTube?' Ollie asked. 'Is this something about
the video Hannah uploaded yesterday?'

Mum nodded.

Hector pulled out his phone slowly and starting
pressing buttons and skimming his fingers across the
screen.

'How bad is it?' Ollie asked Hector.

Hector looked at his phone, then at Ollie, then
at his phone, and then at Hannah, and then at his
phone. 'Okay, so we've had a few views.'

'It can't be that many. YouTube is massive. No
one knows we're there,' Ollie said.

'It's quite a few,' Hector said.

'HOW MANY, HECTOR?' Ollie said, his voice
filled with panic.

'Fourteen million,' Hector replied, thrusting his phone in Ollie's face. 'No wait, I mean sixteen million!'

'What? Don't be stupid, we don't have that many,' Ollie said grabbing the phone.

'We do, which is just mad. I mean there aren't even that many people in the world.'

'What are you talking about, of course there are. There's billions in the world,' Hannah scoffed.

'Oh, like a billion is more than a million!' Hector laughed sarcastically.

'Of course it is,' Hannah laughed. 'Give me the phone. It won't be that many! You see, it's not . . .' she trailed off, '. . .it's now twenty-three million.' Hannah gasped. 'How did you get twenty-three million views?'

'Well, that's what I'd like to know!' shouted Ollie.

'It wasn't me,' Hannah said, putting the phone down. 'I haven't shared it with anyone. Well, except for maybe twenty-seven of my closest friends . . . oh, it might have been me.'

'What if twenty-seven of those people sent it to

twenty-seven of their friends, and so on, and so on?!' Hector yelled. 'That's how these things start. Then before you know it, it all adds up to . . . loads!'

'Oh, perfect. Wait, how did you know, Mum? Did you say TV . . .?' Ollie started.

'Because you're on the news. In fact, so am I; you can hear me yelling on that blinking recording!' Mum shrieked. 'They also said,' Mum added, grabbing a spatula, 'that you might be aliens from the future! Is that true? Because I'll flip you like an egg if it is!!' she screeched.

'No, we're not aliens! Don't be silly!' Ollie snapped.

'Oh good, I was just checking. I didn't think so, but that man on the telly got me all spooked,' Mum said, putting down her kitchen utensil. 'Did you know we're number one around the world?!' she gasped.

'TAKE IT DOWN, OLLIE!' Hector yelled. 'THERE'S A PICTURE OF ME IN A ROBIN COSTUME FOR THE WORLD TO SEE! DO YOU REMEMBER THE PASSWORD? HAVE YOU REMEMBERED IT YET?!'

'No. I think, I think it's got a P in it, or cheese, or both,' Ollie said, pulling out a notepad from his dressing-gown pocket with hundreds of incorrect passwords scribbled on it.

'Then we need to phone them up, find Mr YouTube, and give him a call,' Hector suggested.

'I don't think it's named after a man called YouTube. It's not like it belongs to Dave YouTube, you know,' Ollie cried.

'Oh great, so there's no Dave YouTube; you think it might have cheese in it! Come on man! You're supposed to be the smart one. I'm the funny one. I bring the LOLs and the bants; you need to be the sensible one. Why can't you remember?' Hector shouted.

'It wouldn't matter anyway,' Hannah said, grabbing the phone. 'I've put The Twerpz into

YouTube and seven other versions have popped up. 'No, now twelve . . . even if you could take down the original one, there's still loads up there.'

'It wasn't supposed to be like this. This isn't our music; the cat made it.' Ollie slumped on the floor. There was a moment of silence.

'Sorry . . .?' Hannah said, doing her best non-apologetic apology, '. . . although I don't know why I'm saying sorry.' She shrugged.

'You don't know why?!' Ollie said. 'Because we're all over the Internet thanks to you, we're—'

'Famous? So?' said Hannah.

'What do you mean "So"?' Ollie asked.

'Forgive me if I'm mistaken, but isn't that what you wanted?'

There was a moment of silence from Hector and Ollie. 'She . . . does have a point,' Hector said.

Hannah grabbed Hector's phone. 'You have like millions and millions of thumbs up,' Hannah said, pointing at the screen. 'And reviews. Listen to this: This is the most amazing thing I've heard since sliced bread,' Hannah said, reading out one of the comments. 'How you can hear sliced bread I do not know,' she said dismissively. 'And: Astonishing! I wanna hear more.' Hannah sighed. 'People are idiots.'

'We're famous,' Ollie said, letting the words sink in. 'We're really famous. His eyes met Hector's and then in one glorious moment of pure joy, the two boys went totally berserk.

'We are the most talented duo of all time!' Hector yelled, jumping up and down.

'Duo? You're not really a duo are you?' Hannah said looking at Nigel the cat.

'So, that's okay, our duo just became a threeio.' Hector smiled back.

'A trio,' Ollie whispered to Hector. 'More of a background role for Nigel though.'

'I think you mean foursome!' Mum winked.

'What?' Ollie asked.

'Well, I'm on the record too. I just heard myself; therefore I guess I'm in the band.'

'What?!' Ollie snapped. 'You can't be in the band. You're not in, you're too—'

'Too what?' Ollie's mum said, wafting her spatula

at Ollie. 'Think very carefully before you speak.'

'Too . . . mum-ish to be in a band. You can't just join the band, that's not how it works. Like the way Hannah just can't join *our* band,' Ollie reasoned.

'I want to join the band,' Hannah blurted out. 'Especially after Darren Ledbetter-gate. I don't think I can ever go back to school again!'

'You just want to be in it to annoy me!' Ollie yelled.

'Just so you know, Hannah, I'm cool with it.' Hector winked.

'Hector!' Ollie cried out.

'Why not?' Mum asked. 'Hannah added the cat that made the music that got uploaded.'

'That wriggled and tickled inside her,' Hector said with a grin. 'Sorry, it sounded like that nursery rhyme.'

'I think it'd be a nice thing for us to do as a family,' Mum carried on.

'Look, can we all stop joining our band?' Ollie said, putting his foot down. 'There'll be no one else joining the band!'

'Well, *I'm* not letting *you* be in a band. You're grounded,' Mum said, waggling her eyebrows.

'What?' Ollie snapped.

'Not unless you let Hannah and me in,' Mum said sternly. 'Ooh, what about Dad too?!'

FAMILY AFFAIR

'Okay, okay, Mum, and Hannah I'd like to welcome you to the band. I'm sorry for being mean and saying that you weren't allowed in. You are. So, welcome to The Twerpz,' Ollie said, staring down at his shoes. 'Now, am I ungrounded?' Ollie asked Mum.

'Yes, you need to learn to share with each other. Don't you feel much happier that we're all in the band? It'll be like a great adventure, but instead of it just being you and your best mate, your mum and sister are coming too, and that's better because . . .'

'There's nothing more important than family,' Ollie repeated, the lines having been drilled into him.

'I would especially like to welcome you, Hannah, to the band. I am here for you, happy to help, if you need any advice on being hip, just ask me, Hector, your bandmate.' Hector smiled.

'Keep away from me or I'll snap you like a breadstick,' snapped Hannah.

'Fair play,' Hector said, backing off.

'Right, does anyone else want to be in the band? Nan maybe, a couple of teachers, you know, to keep things really cool and rock and roll.'

'Cut the sarcasm young man, or I'll tell everyone the cat is the chief songwriter.'

'Fine!' Ollie snapped.

At that moment, Dad stormed into the kitchen and demanded, 'Who are The Twerpz? There are fifteen tourists in the rose bed who want their autograph?'

'BING BONG!' the front door bell bonged. 'I'll go and see who it is,' Mum said.

'What did you do, Dad?' Ollie asked.

'I set the hose on them, what do you think I did?'

'Daaaaaad!' Hannah and Ollie groaned.

'Yeaaah, Dad,' Hector said, not wanting to feel left out.

'What?' Dad said, looking confused. 'Did you *not* hear me? There were a load of tourists yelling at me from the rose bed. I nearly filled my not inconsiderable slacks!' Dad cried.

'Daaaaaaad!' everyone cried out in disgust, including Hector.

'Can someone please fill Dad in about how we're the greatest band of all time,' Ollie said, checking out the back window.

'Leave it to me!' Hector announced. 'Ollie and I have known each other for many years; I think it was at the age of five, when performing in a school nativity play—'

'Yeah, the quick version, Hector!' Ollie said hurriedly, spotting another person lurking amongst the runner beans.

'Ollie and I made some music. That music got put out on the internet. We became really famous, and, is it fair to say, regarded as geniuses?' Hector said, looking at Ollie.

'Yep, that's fair,' Ollie agreed.

'What? When did this happen? How long have I been in the shed?' Dad asked.

'Well, it sort of happened overnight, while we were all asleep,' Ollie said, ducking underneath the kitchen window.

'You became famous and geniuses in less than twenty-four hours, while you were asleep?' Dad said, rolling his eyes.

'Yes, I know it's a bit weird, but we are literally overnight successes. I promised I'd ask, but do you want to be in the band too? Apparently anyone and everyone can join.' Ollie smiled in a sort of, well-what-can-you-do fashion.

'Be in your band? What? No!' Dad barked.

'He's going to say it,' Hannah whispered quietly.

'What?' Hector asked.

'It's another sign of a world gone mad,' Dad proclaimed.

'That,' Hannah said.

'We're allowing him to say it once a day now. Any more than that and he has to pay a fine.'

'There's a Sky News truck on our lawn, and one from CNN, and thousands of people yelling "Twerpz" at the house!' Mum said, coming back into the kitchen. 'That was them at the door!'

'How do they know where we live?' Dad asked.

'It's hard to know which one of my twenty-seven closest friends may have betrayed me, but my guess would be that one of them told the TV people,' Hannah said, looking guilty. 'What are we going to do?'

'We need to make a statement. We need to talk

to our fans, tell them to leave us alone, you know, go away a bit,' Ollie said.

'Rightio! Leave it to me!' Mum said, grabbing her rolling pin.

'NO!' Ollie snapped.

'What?'

'You can't go out in your apron waving a rolling pin,' Ollie said, taking charge. 'If we're going to be

rock stars, we need to look like rock stars. Look, I've been wanting this, dreaming about this for years. I know how it works. The first image of us the world sees is not going to be me in my pyjamas, you in your pinny, and Hector in his school uniform.'

'Even though I am rocking it.' Hector grinned at Hannah.

'We need to think about this,' reasoned Ollie.

'But what are we going to wear? All my clothes are at home.' Hector shrugged.

'Don't worry, I've got an idea!' Ollie said. 'A really good one!'

⭐

'Just come out!' Ollie said, banging on the toilet door.

'I don't want to,' Hector said from behind the bathroom door.

'Why not? It's going to be great,' Ollie said, stood in his Batman costume. It was the one from the photo that Hannah had uploaded to YouTube. 'This is number two on the list, mate,' he said, pulling out his Manifesto for World Domination. 'We have number one; the name—granted The Twerpz isn't what I would have chosen, but we're through the looking-glass now. Next comes looking good, followed by three, talking cool. Four was obviously a striking hairstyle and how to spend all the many millions that the band would make.'

'Millions?' Hector asked from behind the toilet door.

'Millions. But it all starts with a name and the look,' replied Ollie encouragingly. I mean yeah, sure his costume smelt a bit musty, and there was a dodgy stain on the front where Ollie had tucked into an egg bap rather too vigorously, but this was their signature look. 'This is our outfit; this is like our "thing". You're just lucky that I had the Robin one here.'

'I don't feel lucky,' Hector's voice quivered. 'This costume is quite tight; I've grown quite a lot since I bought it!'

'We haven't grown that much. Mine still fits me. Yes, it's a little snug in certain places, but we should be fine, as long as we move slowly.'

'Move slowly? We're in a rock band. Moving slowly doesn't sound like rock and roll to me.

WHAAAAAAAAA!'

'What are you doing in there?' asked Ollie. 'You just have to put the costume on, not eat it.'

The door swung open, and despite the fact that Hector was wearing a mask, Ollie could see that he was uncomfortable.

'Wow, you have grown,' Ollie said, taking a step back. 'You see, this is what happens when you eat two breakfasts everyday of your life.'

'I look idiotic.'

'No, no, not idiotic, but . . . iconic!' Ollie said, his voice full of as much encouragement as he could pack in.

'I look like a human icing bag, an icing bag packed with too much icing,' Hector said, looking down at his wobbly, shiny body. 'This is too small. I was eight when I last wore this.'

'Look, trust me, it's fine. I think we look good. We'll just run everywhere, so we're just a blur!' Ollie said helpfully.

'Run?! You want me to run *and* walk slowly. Which is it, Ollie? Because I tell you this, if I run, this whole costume's going to burst with bits of me flying out. Not good bits Ollie, bad bits!'

'Well, somewhere between running slowly and dawdling quickly,' Ollie suggested. 'Look, let's see what Mum and Hannah think.'

Ollie and Hector crept down the stairs, slowly.

Very slowly. One false move and their costumes might well have come to pieces.

'As you can see, Hector and I are dressed as Batman and Robin,' Ollie said as he barged into the living room. I thought this would help us to look like the front cover of our song. It gives us a sense of authenticity, our company logo if you will. As the more observant of you may have noticed, the costumes are a little on the small side. We have grown since the original birthday party when these were debuted a couple of years ago—'

'Four years ago,' Hector confirmed.

'Yep, you could be right. But the tightness of the tights does mean that we are naturally predisposed to walk in a funky manner, as demonstrated by my friend Hector.'

'Ow . . . ow . . . ow . . .' Hector said as he limped in a circle around the living room.

'To the untrained eye, it may look like Hector's in a lot of pain, but if we add some drumbeats behind him, dum-de-dum . . .' Ollie began to replicate a drum machine at this point, 'you will see that actually it's not pain, just cool funky rhythms. We were thinking about maybe a costume for Nigel, but he's a cat, so he's already pretty anonymous. So we decided that Nigel should just be in his cage. We put a bow on it to jazz it up. We can't have the world's greatest songwriter left on his own; he might decide to go and move up the street again! So gang, shoot—what do we think?' Ollie said. 'I will take comments from the floor, once Hannah's stopped laughing. Hannah!'

'I'm sorry, but you look ridiculous. I mean, have you seen yourselves?'

'You were the one who put that picture of us dressed as Batman and Robin on YouTube. You are the reason we're dressed like this! And as you're now in the band, I would like a bit of support,' Ollie replied.

'Ooooh, I could wear an outfit too. I still have that hat from Aunty Marjory's wedding last year. It'd be good to get my money's worth. It was from M&S and it wasn't even in the sale!' Mum said.

'Thank you, little brother, I am having the best day,' Hannah chuckled.

'Mum, what do you think? Can you say something nice, please? Just be honest.'

Mum thought for a second. 'Do you want me to say something nice *or* be honest—I can't do both.'

'Alright, forget it,' Ollie said, rolling his eyes. 'What about you Hannah, what are you going to wear? We have our costumes; Mum has her hat, what about you?'

Hannah thought for a second and then shrugged. 'I dunno. This?' she said, looking at her hoodie and trainers.

'Well fine, it's a little boring, but I suppose it'll do. Anyway, Mum, grab your hat and we can go into the world and claim our fame. I wrote a statement for the press while Hector was busy shoe-horning his way into his tiny costume. It's fairly short, you know, just saying thank you to the fans, now clear off, but nicer than that obviously. Dad, what about you? Are you sure you don't want to be in the band? I mean, everyone else is.'

'No, thank you, it's all tripe!' Dad huffed.

'Thank you, Dad,' Ollie said. 'Let's go.' Ollie held

a tiny piece of paper in his hand with a few scribbled words on it and headed towards the door. This was the moment, the moment that he'd been dreaming of for years, or what felt like years. He'd gone to bed annoyed at what his sister had done and woken up the greatest musician of all time. He took a deep breath, tried to ignore the 'ow, owing' from Hector every time he took a step, and opened the door.

His eyes were immediately blinded by the flash of a thousand flashbulbs. His ears were deafened by the thousands of questions that were being fired in his direction. He'd gone from a no one to superstar in hours. It suddenly felt overwhelming. He looked over at Hector, who was beaming with pride, the pain and wincing had melted away. The noise of a thousand fans, camera crews, and photographers almost knocked him off his feet. Ollie put his hands up to try and quieten the crowd down. It worked. There was an almost immediate silence. It was as if he was a real superhero. He opened his mouth. These were the first words that the world would hear The Twerpz say; they would probably be replayed for all eternity in the rock and roll hall of fame. Should he say fantastic to be here? Or pleased to meet you? In the end, Ollie went with both, sort of.

'PANTASTIC TO BEET YOU!' he yelled out.

Just at that second, the whole house began to vibrate. Suddenly the crowd outside began to scream in terror as they stared up at the sky. That's when the roar began, soft at first but getting louder with every passing heartbeat. Louder and louder until the windows felt like they were about to shatter into a thousand pieces. Like the roof was about to be blown off.

'IT'S THE END!' Dad screamed, hitting the floor at the same time as everyone else. 'THAT'S IT, SHED, HERE I COME!' he shouted, doing a commando crawl along the hall, his hips clicking with every movement.

'IT'S THE ALIENS! THEY'VE COME TO GET THEIR MUSIC BACK! WHERE'S MY RUDDY SPATULA!' Mum cried out in despair.

'Wait, I know what that sound is!' Ollie yelled. It wasn't the end of the world, or an alien invasion. 'It's a helicopter!' Ollie said, standing up. He was right. Parked on the grass was a huge helicopter. Slowly, everyone else did the same. Ollie wiped the dust from his eyes and looked around; the rest of them couldn't help but smile. I mean, it's not every day that a helicopter lands on your lawn. Yes, it may have given Dad's hedge a bit more of a trim than he was anticipating, but they could just buy a new one. Or maybe just move out; live in a mansion with a full-time hedge butler. Perhaps they could have one built out of emeralds in the shape of musical notes.

The helicopter's engines slowed, the doors swung open, and the pilot got out. He looked right at Ollie and waved him over. 'MY EMPLOYER WISHES TO SPEAK TO YOU!' the pilot bellowed.

THE PASSENGER

'YOUR EMPLOYER? WHO'S THAT?' Ollie yelled back.

'BIG RECORDS, SIR!' the man boomed.

Ollie turned round to see Hector, Mum, and even Hannah grinning. Nigel was in his carrycase and had managed to sleep through the entire experience, so there was no way of telling what he thought of this bizarre situation. 'SURE!' Ollie shouted back, like it was the most natural thing in the world. And with that, they all headed towards the helicopter. Ollie had never been in a helicopter before, or become an international rock star; it was turning out to be quite a Saturday morning. By now the crowds had parted providing a natural walkway to the chopper.

'Oh, what about Dad?' Ollie said, turning to Mum.

'Leave him in his shed. It's his happy place,' Mum said. 'Plus he hates heights.'

All of them hopped aboard. Climbing through the doors and into the cabin, once again the engine began to roar. The helicopter rose high above the house. It was then, and only then, that Ollie and Hector could see just how many people there were; there were thousands. There was no way that a few words would have got rid of all those people.

'So,' Hannah started, '"pantastic to beet you"? Do you want to talk about that now?'

'Can we not?' Ollie smiled; even Hannah's sarcasm couldn't dampen his spirit. The helicopter took a sharp right. Ollie's eyes widened as he felt his stomach lurch. Within seconds they lost sight of the houses below, which were replaced with skyscrapers and office blocks as they headed further into the city.

Ollie suddenly felt like he was starring in the movie of his own life. He never thought that his dreams were going to come true. He made a promise to himself there and then that he was going to remember every moment. Maybe he could even play himself in the movie; maybe someone would even turn it into a book. But would anyone believe it?

The skyscrapers began to get higher and higher. There was another twist and a turn and then the helicopter began to slow down. Hector inched himself to the window; it was still very high up and he wasn't used to this sort of thing.

The cabin remained silent; everyone was lost in their own thoughts. They probably all had the same one—*is this really happening?* The helicopter got lower and lower towards the top of the biggest skyscraper in the city. The home of Big Records. Ollie looked out the window. There below them was a helipad, with an H inside a big O. Ollie looked at Hector and grinned.

'It's like they knew we were coming,' Hector said.

A few moments later the helicopter was down. It was like it landed on a big comfy duvet. The blades slowed to a sweeping stop. The pilot clambered out

and opened the door for them. Ollie and Hector were the first out, grabbing their capes so as not to get blown away. Mum helped Hannah out; she was carrying Nigel, who had remained asleep during the entire flight.

'My boss is this way,' a lady said, gesturing them away from the helicopter to a glass lift that was open and ready. Ollie, Hector, Mum, and Hannah walked inside; their legs felt wobbly after the flight. Once in, the doors began to shut. Ollie looked around; there was only one button on the elevator panel. Ollie shrugged and pressed it, and the lift lowered into the heart of Big Records. No one knew who really owned Big Records. Maybe that's why they were the perfect fit for The Twerpz: a mystery boss for a mystery band. It was rumoured that one of the ex-members of the Tweenies, a kids' TV show from the noughties, ploughed all their savings into the company and formed Big Records. Others say it is someone more sinister, a criminal mastermind hell-bent on world domination. Either way, The Twerpz were about to find out. There has only ever been one photograph seen of the boss. It was a blurry black-and-white image of a man, heavyset, chewing on a cigar. He wore sunglasses and had a ponytail. This image would certainly support the second theory. But no one really knew. Big Records was the best and richest record company in the whole world. It had every major artist working for them. They were the biggest and the best for a reason: they paid the most money, and their artists had the most downloads and sold the most records.

'Penthouse Suite,' a robotic voice said.

'OOOOhhhhhh,' everyone said under their breaths. The doors of the lift glided open to reveal a vast marble room with a desk behind it. A man wearing dark glasses gestured them forward. Hesitantly, everyone walked towards what must have been the reception. The receptionist seemed to be shouting right at them, 'GREAT, GREAT, SURE! I MEAN, WHAT DO YOU THINK?'

Ollie was confused. 'Pardon . . .?' he began to say, before realizing that the man was actually wearing an earpiece and was clearly on the phone to someone else.

'YEAH, GOODBYE!' he barked, typing into a tablet as he clicked his Bluetooth device off.

'Hellooooo,' Mum said doing a little wave. 'Erm, we're here to see . . . actually who are we seeing?'

The receptionist, looking bored, pointed the way through to the next room without even looking up from the tablet. The gang all looked at each other and walked through. The view took their breath away. There was a huge window with a view of the city, the city they'd been flying over just a few minutes ago. The office was the size of Ollie's house, maybe even the size of two of his houses. A marble floor clinked and tinkled with every footstep, and at the end of the room sat a huge desk. It was as wide as four ping-pong tables laid end-to-end. On it sat a small computer and lamp. Or maybe it was a huge computer; it was hard to tell as the place was so big. There was also a huge chair. It was facing the other way, and as they got nearer, they could hear the gruff voice of a man. He was clearly on the phone, talking while staring at what must have been fifty, maybe even one hundred gold and platinum discs hanging on the wall. Suddenly everyone felt nervous, like they were in a very grown-up world. The gruff voice stopped talking, like he'd heard their footsteps. Ollie could just make out the words, 'Got to go . . . they're here.' The phone was put down and slowly the chair turned, and there was the man, the one that everyone had seen on TV, in the one and only photo of the boss of Big Records. He had dark glasses and a ponytail, thick stubble, and a mean-looking mouth.

Ollie greeted him with a smile that soon disappeared when he saw how annoyed the man looked.

'So, you want to be in the music business do you? Well, I have an offer that you can't refuse. We're looking for a band just like you. In fact, I can tell you for certain that it will be you. No one. Ever. Turns. Us. Down,' he said, handing them what presumably were contracts. Everyone suddenly felt uneasy.

'And . . . er . . . if we don't want to do it?' Hector asked, saying aloud what everyone was thinking.

'Then your career will be over. You'll be finished. Not just with me, but with everyone forever. When I said sign these, it wasn't a question you know . . .' He smiled a terrifying smile and let out a barrelling laugh like his chest was made of gravel.

'Well, there's no need to be so mean, Julian!' a voice suddenly interrupted, shattering the uncomfortable silence. At that second, from behind the wall that had all the many gold discs, a secret door opened. There stood a little old lady, and I mean little—she could have only been about five foot tall at the most. She wore a little pair of specs, pearl earrings, a big beaded necklace, and she was clutching a shiny leather handbag—the sort that almost certainly contained either knitting or Murray Mints, but probably both. She ushered the heavyset man, who apparently was called Julian, out of the chair, took a seat, and swapped her specs over to read the paperwork. Things had just got weird. Well, it was already pretty weird; but things had just got much, *much* weirder.

'I'm sorry, who are you?' Mum said, speaking for the group.

'Oh, I'm Doris,' she said, smiling.

'Er, great,' Ollie said. 'Doris.'

Everyone took a second, too dumbstruck to talk.

'Doris?' Ollie asked.

'Yes poppet?' she said, looking up.

'Who are you?' Mum asked again.

'Oh, you mean what do I do?' she said, lifting

up the contract and holding it as far away as her little arms would allow so it would get into focus. 'I'm the head of Big Records, lovely. Nice outfits,' she said, making a few notes on the pieces of paper. Everyone let out a small nervous chuckle. Doris gave a warm smile.

'Well, then who's this big chap?' Hannah asked.

'He just pretends to be the boss, for appearances' sake. I'm so sorry he was rude. Julian, I've told you about that,' Doris scolded.

'Sorry Doris. I was just worried they wouldn't sign the contracts and become part of Big, you know, part of our one big happy family.' He shrugged.

'Julian is very enthusiastic,' she said. 'Don't worry chuck, they'll join, I'm sure.'

'How do you know?' Ollie asked.

'Because I can change your life,' she said, looking perplexed. 'Isn't that why anyone's in a band, because they want to be someone, or something else?' she said. 'Here, let me give the tour—Julian, you can go and have your lunch.'

'Thanks, Doris,' he said, grabbing a pasty out of

the desk drawer along with a banana milkshake, and strolling towards the lift.

'Well, come on dearies,' Doris said, ushering the family and Hector through the secret door.

'I use Julian to pretend to be the head of Big Records, the way those nasty dictators use look-alikes. It makes for a better image, you know, a big scary boss.' Doris did her best big scary face. 'I think Julian is the fourth one we've had. Normally they come in for a few years, pretend to be the boss, you know, just in case there are any photographers around,' Doris said, leading the gang through a corridor to a high-tech recording studio. It was like they were entering a secret world. 'So this is the hit factory, everything from hip-hop to death metal and all in between. We at Big Records only take the best and most innovative musical acts—'

Ollie and Hector looked at each other and grinned, before looking down at the cat. That sort of wiped the smile from both their faces.

'Do you think we should tell her about Nigel?' Hector whispered to Ollie.

'Hector, this is our chance of the big time! Anyway, do you really think she would believe us if we told her the truth?' Ollie mouthed back.

'I guess it would be silly to let a little thing like having zero musical talent stop us from becoming total rock stars,' Hector smirked.

'Exactly! I'm not sure Doris would even care. I mean, she's not who she says she is. She has Julian; that makes her a Nigel in human form.'

In the studio there were a couple of techie guys mixing some sort of grime album. 'You need to crank up the bass dearies,' Doris said sweetly. 'You know I want people's noses to bleed when they hear it,' she said, offering them a sucky sweet as a treat.

'I told you!' one said to the other.

'Thanks Doris,' the other said, taking a sweet.

'So, I started Big Records many years ago. I was a tea girl back in the music industry in the 70s. I was always around the place, dishing out tea, listening to how things were run. From the recording studio, to the boardroom, it's amazing the things people will say when you're invisible. Being a tea lady meant that I was there all the time, but no one noticed me. Well, when my Frank passed on, gawd rest his soul, he left me a bit of money that he'd gathered over the years from his winnings on the Premium Bonds, and I thought, well, there's two things I could do: I could sit at home, watching *Countdown* and drinking tea, or I could put my money into a multi-platform digital music provider, with a 360-degree content driving ethos. So I thought I'd do that—plus my spelling is terrible. I used all that industry knowledge to spot a gap in the market and develop a record company that is also a TV business, an app, and a streaming service. So, hands up who wants to be the biggest rock stars in the world?'

Everyone put their hands up.

'Now, you two are the songwriters, aren't you?' Doris said, looking at Ollie and Hector. 'Here's your contract.'

Ollie and Hector looked at each other and grinned. 'I can't believe it!' Ollie beamed.

'Nor me!' Hector laughed.

'Well—' Doris began.

'This is what we always wanted,' Ollie said, grabbing the pen from Doris's hand and scrawling his signature across the dotted line before handing it to Hector who did the same.

'I really think—' Doris tried to interrupt.

'WE DID IT!' Ollie shrieked. 'WE ACTUALLY DID IT—WE'RE GOING TO BE ROCK STARS!!!'

They laughed and sang and jumped around!

'Well, normally people like to read the contract first,' Doris said, finally getting her words out. 'Or get a lawyer to look at it. But hey, we're all in it now. There's no turning back.'

Ollie stopped jumping up and down. 'I'm sure it's all fine.'

'Oh, what does this bit mean?' Hannah asked, looking at the paper that Ollie and Hector had just signed.

'Oh, that? It just says that any fraudulent behaviour on your part cancels the contract. For example, if you two claimed to have written the song but actually it turned out that you stole it from someone else, the whole agreement becomes worthless and you don't get a penny. There was once a band many moons ago, who said that they wrote the songs; it turned out that it was the band's mum. Of course, once that came out they were finished, they lost all credibility. It'd be like . . . a cat writing the song. It would instantly become worthless.' Doris laughed. 'Now, champagne? No, even better, tea! I'll get some biscuits too! Oh, Hannah and Mrs Thickett, can you sign it too?' Doris said, leaving the studio.

Ollie looked at the scribbled contract. 'I hereby declare that The Twerpz are the songwriters of the above music?'

'Is it fraud? Have we just committed fraud?' Hector asked. 'It feels like we might have just claimed to be the writers of a song we didn't write.'

'What are we going to do?' Hannah said. 'If anyone finds out you didn't write the song, you'll be finished.'

'And if we tell the truth, our dreams will be over before they even get started,' Ollie pleaded. 'Listen, it'll be fine.' Ollie smiled, having landed from cloud nine with a thud. 'I'm not going to tell, and as long as no one else does we'll be fine.'

'What about Nigel?' Hector whispered.

'Okay, Nigel, will you tell?' Ollie asked. There was silence. 'Nigel's all good,' Ollie said reassuringly.

'Just checking. I mean, you never know, I'm sure that it's only a matter of time before someone invents a talking cat.'

'It's fraud!' Hannah whispered. 'What are you going to do when . . . we have to write an entire album?!' Hannah said, looking at the contract.

'We can do it. We have each other. We have Nigel. Maybe he can do it again. Maybe it won't work, but we have to try, don't we?' Ollie pleaded to the rest of the band.

Hannah grabbed the pen off Hector and shook her head. 'I've got a bad feeling about this.'

MONEY, MONEY, MONEY

'So here's the plan,' Doris said, bursting back into the studio with a tray of goodies. 'I want to do concerts, TV shows; I'm talking a global audience of billions, interviews, the whole works. I've never seen so many hits on YouTube in such a short time. I mean, what are we up to now?' Doris said, pulling out her phone. 'Seven hundred million. We'll put your music up for download, and even if a tenth of the people who watched you on YouTube download your song, buy a T-shirt or come and see you in concert— you'll all be millionaires by the end of this week. I'm thinking we should have a big concert tomorrow night. We'll put it on the internet as well as all the TV channels. It'll be a huge event, to announce your arrival to the music world. This secret band and their big unveiling. Are you okay with playing on TV?'

'Play? On TV? In front of the world?' Ollie asked, realizing what this meant. How were they supposed to play a song that was an accident? It'd be like spilling a load of paint on the carpet and someone asking you to do it again with exactly the same results. How do you recreate something as random as Nigel going wild and running over your keyboard?

'It's a lot to take in. Listen, we have a penthouse apartment,' Doris said, pointing at the door on the other side of the office, 'where you can all go and talk it over, have a jam, rehearse a bit. We can get you some instruments, in fact anything you need we can give you, now that you're part of the team.'

'And if we didn't want to play tomorrow?' Hannah asked nervously, also realizing what a pickle they were in.

'Oh well, you know, you sort of have to, it's all

there,' Doris said, pointing at the contract. 'If you don't, I'll just sue you for lots of money, and I mean *millions*.' Doris winked. 'Ha! You lot are sooooo funny, "what if we don't want to play on TV . . ."' Doris said, pretending as if the whole thing was a joke. Just at that second, Doris's phone buzzed. 'Ooh, got to go. Beyoncé's having a meltdown. I best get in there and make sure she's okay. Rock stars, eh?!' Doris chuckled. 'Enjoy the apartment and I'll see you later!' she said, grabbing a couple of biscuits as she left.

⭐

'Right,' Ollie said, looking at the Doris-less room. 'Anyone else feel scared?'

Everyone put their hand up, including Ollie.

'So, on the bright side, we could all be millionaires by the end of the week. On the downside, we have to play a song that we didn't write and don't know how to play.'

'In front of a TV audience that will probably be billions!' Hector added.

'Thank you, I almost forgot that,' Ollie said.

'And we have essentially committed fraud by signing a contract saying that we wrote the song, when it was Nigel the cat,' Mum also added.

'Again, thanks, you guys. What would I do without my bandmates?' Ollie sighed.

'Oh, what do I do in the band by the way? I've been meaning to ask,' said Mum.

'Oh yeah, what do I do?' Hannah asked.

'Right, okay, so I play keyboard and sing. Hector is on guitar and sort of sings a bit. Mum, how do you feel about maracas?'

'I feel good,' Mum said, grinning.

'Stand at the back, shake some maracas, and then at the end you shout "keep that noise down!" Okay?' Ollie said.

'Yes, boss,' Mum saluted.

'Hannah,' Ollie said narrowing his eyes.

'Yeeeees?' Hannah replied.

'I want you to be backing singer,' Ollie said, thinking on his feet. 'You can stand and sing "oh yeah" every so often, and sort of dance a bit . . . you know, look cool. Is that something you can do?'

Ollie asked.

'Moving and saying two words every so often? Yep, I think I'll be fine. What key are we singing in? Major? Minor? Are we going for C, D or E? ' Hannah asked.

Ollie paused for a second thinking and said, 'Pick your favourite.'

'And Nigel?' Hannah asked.

'What about him?' Ollie said.

'Well, he's in the band; he kind of needs to be there too. What's he going to play?' Hannah asked.

'Are you serious? "What's he going to play?" What would you have him play? Cello? Viola? Perhaps he could be like a one-man band, you know, tie a couple of cymbals to his knees and strap a kazoo to his fury face. What about that?' Ollie said, losing his cool. 'Nigel stays with us at all times. We may need him!'

'Well, there's no need for that tone.' Hannah sniffed.

'I AM IN CASE YOU HADN'T NOTICED UNDER QUITE A LOT OF PRESSURE AT THE MOMENT. I HAVE TO TEACH YOU ALL A

SONG I HAVEN'T LEARNT YET AND THE
ONLY PERSON WHO KNOWS THE SONG IS
CURRENTLY LICKING HIS OWN BOTTOM.'

'NO, I'M NOT!' Hector yelled. 'I was just having
a scratch.'

'No, not you. Nigel,' Ollie explained.

'Oh yeah,' Hector said, nodding. 'Alright, what
about this for a plan—why don't we see if we can get
him to teach us how to play?' Hector suggested.

'What?' Ollie snapped.

'I don't mean literally. I mean, let's see if we can
get him to do it again. Then we can see how he does it,
you know, learn from the master, recreate his sound.'

'How?' Ollie asked.

'Well, why don't we just recreate your bedroom,
Ollie? That way we can recreate the moment. Doris
did say we could order anything we needed,' Hector
said, reaching for the penthouse telephone with a
cheeky glint in his eye.

'Er, yes, hello,' Julian said, picking up his phone.
'Er, yes, Big Records are paying for everything. Doris
said you can have whatever you want—why? Pardon,

can you say that again?'

Hector repeated his request. 'A bag of cat nip, thirty-two tins of tuna, a ball of wool, a dangly fish on the end of a small novelty fishing rod, a bunk bed, several posters of Tottenham Hotspur players past and present, a laundry basket full of old socks, a Yamaha keyboard, electric guitar, recorder, mics, and a laptop. Oh, and seven pizzas with a variety of toppings. Oh yeah, and a tailor,' Hector said, pulling a wedgie out of his tights.

'We didn't have any pizza in my room that day,' Ollie said.

'I know. It's dinner time. Do you guys want anything?' Hector asked.

'That's not all for you?!' Mum shouted in horror.

'No ... obviously,' Hector quickly said. Although it was obvious that he'd ordered them for himself.

Julian finished noting down the order list. 'That's fine, give me a few minutes. We'll send it up.'

Within thirty minutes and with a lot of shifting of very heavy and expensive furniture from the apartment it looked a bit like Ollie's bedroom, a bedroom within a bedroom if you like. Cat treats were primed, ready to get Nigel in the mood. The keyboard was switched on. Hector had his recorder. The samba drumbeat was ready to drop. Everyone was given a line of the song to say.

'Right, are we ready?! GOOOOOOO!' Ollie yelled. The F was blown on the recorder, there was some bobbing and dancing and the drumbeat began. Strange words were said while Mum and Hannah cajoled Nigel, who looked around at the strange yet familiar setting and promptly went to sleep where he was standing. Ollie stopped the drumbeat and signalled to the others to stop singing and dancing.

'This is going to be harder than I thought,' Hector said, putting his hands on his hips.

'Is there something missing?' Hannah asked.

'I know! A dog. I had a dog on my hoodie. I wonder if that got his blood going?' Hector asked.

'You could be right,' Ollie said. 'We can't wait for them to get a dog.'

'Mrs T, empty out your handbag. I've had an even better idea . . .'

Within seconds, and with the help of an eyeliner and some digestive biscuits taped to his head to represent ears, Hector looked like a dog. Not a very good dog, but if you squinted, turned down the lights and had a really good imagination, he looked like a dog. Nigel opened his eyes, slowly, to see Hector on his hands and knees crawling towards him, growling and wagging his tail. And by tail, I mean a rolled-up shower mat. All the while Mum, Ollie, and Hannah chanted the lyrics to their song.

'Here are your pizzas!' The door suddenly opened. There was Julian with armfuls of pizza boxes. He took one look at the bizarre scene, calmly put the boxes down, and tutted 'rock stars' under his breath.

'Oh look, it's working! Look who's up!' Hannah said, pointing at Nigel who was staring at Hector, eyes wide open. In fact his eyes were a little too open!

'Now, calm down Nigel.

Er, Hector, I think you're scaring him. Maybe stop the growling.'

'Nah, it'll be fine,' Hector said.

Nigel's tail began to bristle and shake.

'Hector!' Hannah yelled. 'Nigel looks very unhappy.'

'Don't be silly, he's just getting ready to play,' Hector laughed.

But Nigel had a wild look in his eye; there was no stopping him now. He was primed and ready to go.

'Nigel! NO!' everyone yelled.

NERVOUSLY

Well, at least Hector and the rest of the band had confirmed what it was that got Nigel's creative juices going; it was the sight and sound of a dog. The band watched in horror as Nigel launched into his fifteenth circuit of the apartment, approaching speeds of forty miles an hour, scratching, hissing, and destroying anything in his way.

'I've never seen a cat pull a TV off the wall. I mean, that's pretty impressive,' Ollie said, holding a chair in front of his body by way of protection.

'That's true, but can we talk about the

power-to-weight ratio of the cat and his core strength another time? I mean, as much fun as it is, I think maybe we should concentrate on trying to catch Nigel at this moment in time,' Hannah said, taking up the chase. 'NO Nigel, not the Victorian teaset!' But it was too late. That, along with the contents of the minibar, the small but useful kettle, and the Corby trouser press had all been destroyed in the wake of Nigel the rampaging cat.

'This is all your fault, Hector!' Hannah yelled out.

'I know!' Hector yelled, standing on top of the bed using a tea tray like a shield.

'I've got an idea,' Mum said, looking around. She spotted the laundry basket in the corner. To walk over to it would be dangerous, especially with the speed Nigel was circuiting. He may well take Mum's legs off. Seeing the chandelier in the middle of the room, Mum grabbed a rope tie from one of the many dressing-gowns strewn around the suite. She lassoed it onto the chandelier, and in one swoop, swung over to the other side of the room, grabbed the laundry basket, commando-rolled into Nigel's path, and

scooped him up, caging him like the wild beast he was.

'Now that was impressive!' Hannah laughed.

'Well, I knew my SAS training would have a purpose one day,' replied Mum.

'You were in the SAS?' Hector asked.

'Yeah, it was just a Saturday job until the cleaning business took off,' Mum panted. 'Blimey, do you think Doris will notice?' she said, looking around the room.

Everyone took a moment to settle down before attention turned to the damage. Then there was a loud thumping at the door.

'Oh my word, what are we going to do? I mean look at this place,' Hector said.

'I think we better just come clean and own up,' Ollie said. He walked over to the door and pulled the door handle, which came off in his hand. 'How does a cat destroy a door knob?!' Ollie forced open the door and gave a smile to Julian, several other assistants, and a worried-looking Doris, who had gathered outside on hearing the hullabaloo inside the apartment.

'Er, sorry Doris,' Hector said, looking guilty. 'It was my fault. I think I spooked Nigel.'

'Well, dressing as a giant biscuit dog will do that to a cat,' Doris said, inspecting the damage.

'Look, we'll pay for any damages,' Ollie said.

'Oh, who cares? I'M RICH!' Doris smiled. 'People, can you fix this mess?' she said to her team, who sprang into action. 'How did the jam go?' Doris asked.

'Getting there, you know,' Ollie said. 'Just a bit of fine-tuning, that's all.'

'Oh well, I'll leave you to it. I know how you rock and roll bands like to be up the entire night rehearsing. I, on the other hand, like to be at home in a comfy chair knitting by 7 *p.m.* See you tomorrow, and don't party too hard! The cars will be here to pick you up at 8 *a.m.*,' Doris said, winking and waving. 'These guys will look after you. Until tomorrow, byeeee!' Doris said before waddling off.

'Right then, so there's nothing left to do but pull an all-nighter. No one is leaving this place until we've learnt the song off by heart,' Ollie whispered to the others.

⭐

BONNNNNNG!

'I'm awake!' Hector yelled, having been asleep.

'What time is it?' he said, trying to open his eyes.

'6 *a.m.*!' Ollie snapped.

'There's a 6 *a.m.*, as in the morning?!' Hector said, looking shocked. 'I thought it just went from midnight to morning. Who knew there was a six in the morning? Did you know?' Hector asked Hannah who nodded wearily.

'Mrs T?' Hector asked.

'Oh, for goodness' sake, we all knew. We all know that the numbers start again at midnight. We also all know that a billion is more than a million, and you'd know it too if you occasionally stopped talking and listened for once!' Ollie snapped. 'Like you'd also know that you should play an F at that bit, not whatever it was that you were playing!' he yelled.

'It was an H,' Hector whispered.

'There is no H. It doesn't go up to H. It stops at F!' Ollie shouted.

'G,' Hannah added quietly.

'G! I meant G!' Ollie said, rubbing his face with his hands. 'We have been up all night. I need you all to pay attention and play the song. All we have to do is play the song!'

'How can we play it when the notes you're asking us to play don't exist? And that bit halfway through, when it gets slowed down and reversed, how on earth do you suggest we play that bit?!' Hannah yelled back.

Ollie took a deep breath, got up from his keyboard and began to walk around the plush apartment that sat at the top of Big Records. His head was heavy and thick after an entire night spent trying to learn the band's one and only song. The morning light was breaking over the skyscrapers to the east of the city. The sky was a pretty mixture of blues and gold; it looked like a giant 3D watercolour painting. It was amazing, but no one felt able to appreciate it, as it wasn't just the sun that was dawning in the apartment, it was the realization that they, The Twerpz, were to perform in front of the world later on that day. It was to be a huge event and it already had everyone buzzing. It was all over the news and social media outlets. The rich and famous were all desperate for tickets. Kanye West had sent Hector at least fifteen Instagram requests since dinner, all of which Hector declined, mostly because he thought Kanye West was a train station. The gang had had a power nap somewhere around 3 *a.m.*, for about an hour, but then it was up and back to work. Ollie took a deep breath and, despite feeling the tension and resentment in the room, he said the most feared words in the English language: 'From the top.'

'Oh no more, please, please stop. I've never had a million pounds before,' Mum declared, 'but it really can't be worth all this pain and heartache. I can't take it any more. Please, just no more "from the top". I mean, it just doesn't make sense. It's not like trying to learn a song; it doesn't make sense as a song. It's just a load of noise!' They had been listening over and over to the song that Hannah had uploaded to YouTube, trying to listen and work out what Nigel had done. Which buttons did he press, in what order, but it was impossible. Imagine trying to phone your friend, but you don't have their phone number. Imagine if you just dialled eleven numbers until you found the right one. That was the undertaking they were trying to achieve. It was impossible.

'What are we going to do?' Hannah asked.

'Why don't we just tell Doris, tell her the truth?' Mum suggested.

'Tell me the truth about what?' Doris said, wandering into the apartment. 'Sorry to interrupt. I know this is your place, but I was up early this morning, so I thought I'd pop in and say hi. So does someone want to explain what's going on? Is there a problem with tonight's show?'

Ollie looked around at his friends, and his mum and sister; they all looked pale, sick with worry and tiredness. 'Yes, we shouldn't be on TV, we don't deserve it,' Ollie started.

Just at that second Doris's phone rang out, the ringtone of *There'll be Bluebirds over the White Cliffs of Dover*. 'Hello, yes?' Doris said, answering the phone. As she listened, she mouthed the word 'Sorry' to the band. 'What, the sound's not good enough?' she said down the phone. 'It's the venue,' she mouthed again. 'There's a problem with the sound. They'll have to mime the song? Oh yes, that's fine. I'm sure we can do that,' Doris said, hanging up. 'The sound system's playing up, so we'll have the music as a backing track and you can sing over the top.' Doris smiled. 'I hope that's okay.'

'We don't have to play, just say a few words . . . I mean sing our brilliant song?' Ollie said, smiling.

'Phew!' Mum said, collapsing back onto the sofa.

'Now, what did you want to tell me?' asked Doris. 'Something about the truth, about what you deserve?'

'Er,' Ollie replied.

'What Ollie was trying to say is that we don't feel able to express how happy we are to be given this chance. That's the truth,' Hector said, covering their tracks.

'Oh, no need. Right, cars will be here soon, so get some breakfast and then off to the gig.'

'THERE'LL BE BLUEBIRDS OVER,' Doris's phone rang out.

'Sorry,' Doris said, answering her phone. 'Oh Kanye, please stop calling, you just sound needy. Well I know you want tickets,' Doris said, leaving the band alone again.

'Uuuuhhh,' everyone groaned with relief before

collapsing on sofas, chairs or anywhere that was comfortable.

Ollie hung his head in shame, took a deep breath and readied himself for an apology. 'Right, I think it's only right that I apologize, especially to you Hector. I snapped. I yelled. I shouldn't have done it. It was wrong. I was a fool. I just let it all get on top of me, and the real truth is I couldn't have done this without you. Or you, Hannah. I wouldn't want to do it without any of you. It's just so important to me. It means the world to me to do this and to do this with you guys as well. I guess what I'm trying to say is, I love you. You're my best friend and my family. You're the most important thing in my life. Where would I be without you guys? So, I'm sorry. What say we put this behind us? It's so lovely that I can say this to you, and how you're listening to me as I share what's inside my heart with you. I think that things will never be the same after this moment. So having finally said all that, who wants some breakfast and maybe a hug too?' Ollie smiled a contented smile. But there were no hugs, only silence. Ollie looked up and saw Hannah, Hector, and Mum, fast asleep and snoring away. 'Oh, that's just typical isn't it?' Ollie sighed.

THE SHOW MUST GO ON

A few minutes' sleep later, after a hot shower and breakfast—or in Hector's case several breakfasts—the band were ready. Doris had got the band some new clothes. Hector and Ollie were still in the Batman and Robin costumes, but this time they fitted and were made of a decent material too, not the stuff that kept giving Ollie and Hector static electric shocks every time they touched each other. Finally they felt ready for the day. The fact all they had to do was pretend to play musical instruments and sing live was fine; well, maybe not fine, but infinitely more preferable than trying to play music that didn't make any sense. The lyrics were few and far between anyway. I mean, who was really going to notice the odd 'Yeah baby' in the wrong place?

Doris had arranged for a car to pick the band up from the front of Big Records' offices to take them to the concert. A gang of minders had escorted the band down the stairs and out the front door. Doris, of course, was nowhere to be seen; she took her secret life very seriously. Outside, cameras flashed and a crowd of hundreds of people stood with their back to the band so that they could take the perfect selfie. The band may have been exhausted but a sudden adrenalin shock, like having hundreds of people calling your name, put paid to that. It felt like a dream that had come to life. Six burly minders pushed camera crews and fans out of the way so the band could be put into their giant limo with blacked-out windows; although the anonymity of the windows was sort of cancelled out by the fact that the car had 'The Twerpz—the greatest band of all time!' written in gold lettering on the side. The limo began to move away from the kerb and through the town.

'Does anyone know where we're going? I was so busy practising for the concert that I forgot to ask where it was,' said Ollie.

'The Royal Albert Hall,' one of the minders said.

'Oh, how do you know that?' Hector asked. The minder smiled at Hector before pulling his own face off.

'ARGGGGGHHHHH!' everyone yelled.

'Doris, can you stop doing that?' Ollie cried out.

'Sorry dearies, I thought you knew it was me.'

'How on earth did you disguise yourself as a six-foot bodyguard?' Hannah asked.

'What can I say; make-up today is very good. Anyway, you're playing at the Royal Albert Hall!'

'No way!' Mum shrieked.

'REALLY?!' Ollie and Hannah called out.

'Is that the pub by the sofa shop?' Hector asked.

'No, the Albert Hall, the one on the TV,' Ollie snapped.

'Oh, cool,' Hector said, pretending to know what it was. 'How many people does it hold?'

'Nearly six thousand,' Doris said.

'Whoa, that's a lot,' Ollie gulped.

'Yep, it sure is. That's just people physically there. We've sold it to Facebook, to YouTube, to Twitter. Everyone will be streaming it.'

'Yes, speaking of the show, we only have one song, *Cat Attack*. It seems a lot of effort just for one song. What I'm saying is, it will be a very short concert,' Ollie said, looking concerned.

'Big intro, walk on, lights go black, lots of screaming, then the drums kick in. We can eke that out for three minutes. The lights come on, you sing and stuff, the lights go out; the music comes on again, the lights go out, everyone thinks you're finished, then the music comes on again, there's a big roar, then the lights go out. Do that about six times, big applause at the end, maybe some pyrotechnics and that will probably be about half an hour.' Doris smiled. 'So that's fine. This is your big arrival on the world stage; you could literally go in there and read a shopping list and they'd probably go bonkers.'

'Shopping list?' Hector asked. 'Well, that's the second single sorted.' He grinned.

'Well, okay, it's maybe a little more complicated than that, but they're there to see you,' Doris replied.

The limo swooped through the streets past the front of the hall, although it looked more like a campsite than the entrance to a grand concert venue; such was the amount of people who'd been queuing overnight in order to make sure they got their tickets for the big event. Ollie glimpsed the crowds as he zoomed past. There were people of all ages; some with homemade posters, flags, T-shirts—all of which had 'The Twerpz' written on them. There were people with stalls selling scarfs and T-shirts. It was like a cross between a football match and a carnival. It all felt so unreal. How had Ollie and his band gone from not having a song, or even a name, to being the most famous band in the world in just a couple of days? Hannah uploading the song to YouTube felt like such a long time ago; if Ollie were told it was last month he could almost have believed it.

Ollie looked over at Nigel. He was still trying to process how he felt about it all. Sure it was Nigel's song; he'd made it. Was that an amazing thing, or was it utterly ridiculous? Ollie imagined what would happen if the world knew the truth. Would everyone have a great big laugh, or would they think that Ollie was making fun of them? Maybe it was the world making fun of them? The music that Hannah uploaded was certainly different—Mum had hated it. But did that mean it was bad? I'm sure there were people who thought The Beatles were just making a racket and that it wasn't proper music. Perhaps the world was ready for this new art, created by animals and adored by the public. Ollie's head started to spin trying to unravel it all. He shook his head and snapped himself out of his daydream as they pulled up to the backstage entrance. A host of security guards waved the car through to a secure area so that they could park and depart the limo in peace.

'This way!' Doris said, reattaching her disguise head. She led the band through a maze of corridors before coming out into the middle of the arena. There was an audible gasp as everyone took in the sight. It was huge, a giant circle that seemed to go on forever in every direction. Ollie's belly bubbled and his knees went weak.

'And this is going to be full is it?' Hannah asked, her voice weak and trembling.

'Yep,' said Doris.

'And where will we be?' Mum asked.

'On the stage over there,' Doris said, pointing down the other end of the hall. Everyone turned round and squinted at the stage that seemed so small from where they were standing.

'Crikey. I won't lie to you Doris, the most people I've ever performed in front of was at the nativity play a couple of years ago. I only had one line and it didn't go well—I messed it up, tripped, and ended up toe-poking the baby Jesus into the third row,' Hector said seriously.

'I should point out that the baby Jesus was being played by a doll; no real children were injured,' Ollie added.

'This is the job,' Doris said. 'The cars, the money, the lifestyle, it's all great—and you get rewarded handsomely for being successful—but when it comes down to it, you're here to perform, and I can't help you with that. But, what I do know is that you'll be fine. You have each other, and the crowd will be so hyper that when you come out, it'll be so loud that no one will notice any mistakes. All you have to do is sing and move about a bit. I mean, it is your song, so you should know it off by heart,' Doris advised.

Everyone looked at each other and nodded. She was right. I mean it was just larking about on a stage with a microphone. It's not like they had to go deep-sea diving for sunken treasure, or climb the highest mountain in the world.

The next few hours were spent standing in front of microphones, doing sound checks, making sure the lighting was working, making sure that the cameras that were going to carry the live feed were all in the right place. The checks and double checks seemed to be endless. Doris took the band backstage to get some peace and quiet and so that they could get ready for the big show. Although it was very scary, everyone felt safe around Doris, like it was all going to be okay. She would make sure that they had everything they needed and tell them that they were going to be alright—apart from the occasional moments when she ripped off her own face, it was like have your favourite granny there.

'It's time!' Doris said, looking at her watch. The band were in their costumes. Everyone was fed, watered, and feeling pretty good. Rehearsals had gone well, they'd practised the song with all of Doris's changes, and it had all been great. They even enjoyed it! The venue seemed to shrink in their minds as the afternoon went on and they got more used to their surroundings.

'Is Dad coming?' Ollie asked Mum.

'He says he's going to watch it on the TV. He doesn't want to leave the shed in case anyone else comes knocking. He's been power-hosing all day, blasting tourists out from behind the shrubs. To be honest, I think he's having a whale of a time,' Mum said. 'He did say he doesn't understand any of it, but he's very proud of you,' she added, grinning.

'My lot are out there somewhere,' Hector said, peeking behind the curtain just off stage. 'Mum said she'd be wearing a blue top, so look out for someone with a blue top on.' Everyone nodded back. There must have been about two thousand people wearing blue, but this wasn't the time to point this out to Hector. Ollie took a deep breath, to get him in the zone.

'You're going to be fine,' Doris said, noting that Ollie suddenly seemed quite small in this big world. 'This is what you were born to do.' She smiled at Ollie. Ollie nodded and was about to smile back, when a hand shoved him forward.

'You're on!' a man wearing a headset barked, ushering the band to their place.

The lights were now completely out. The crowd let out a huge gut-rumbling cheer. The excitement was almost tangible. You could feel the nervousness in the air. Ollie could just about see his keyboard in front of him. Over to his right, Hector was standing looking absolutely terrified. To his left, Hannah was also looking scared, and behind him was Mum looking completely the wrong way. 'This way!' Ollie whispered, except it's not a whisper when the microphone is on. The sound thundered around the venue, and the crowd let out another enormous cheer. 'This waaaaaaay to funky town,' Ollie quickly added to cover his tracks. 'Are you ready to rock?!' he yelled, improvising. But it didn't feel strange or awkward; it felt like it was meant to be. Doris was right; this was exactly what he was put on this earth to do. Suddenly the samba beats started to thump and the crowd began to jump. The spotlight hit Ollie between the eyes. There was a roar from the crowd, but because the venue was so large it took a second or two for the wave of sound to hit him. Maybe he was just in the moment, or perhaps he felt protected by the Batman costume; whatever it was, he felt completely at home, like he was in complete control. The audience was looking at him expectantly, so he raised an arm and yelled, 'HEEEEELLLO LONDON! WE ARE . . .?' Then he cupped his hand to his ear

and the crowd shouted back, 'THHHHEEEEE
TWWWEEEEEERPZZZZZZ!'

Ollie looked over at Mum who was finally facing
the right way as she shook her maracas. Hannah
was wiggling around, and Hector was strumming
his guitar, not in time with the music, but he was
strumming it at least.

'Caaaaaaaat attack!' Hector cried.

'Someone fetch the mum!' Ollie sang.

'Yoooooooooow!' Hannah whooped.

'The sound's too loud—drop the beat!' Ollie yelled out again while dancing around.

'I can't! I won't!' Hector bellowed.

'Go, go, GOOOOO!' Hannah cried.

'Oh baby!!' everyone sang.

'Cat attack! Cat attack!' Hector shouted.

This went on for several more minutes until finally the lights came down and they ended to huge cheers and applause. Ollie looked round at everyone; they had joined him at the front of the stage so that they could all take a bow. 'Thank you, thank you!' Ollie said, showing his appreciation.

'We've been magnificent. You've been The Twerpz!' Hector yelled in the mic. 'No wait, I mean that but the other way round!' he said, trying to explain before Ollie grabbed the mic off him.

'Leave the speaking to me,' Ollie said, grinning. Then the lights went down, and they were ushered offstage. It was all over. They'd done it, they'd managed to do their first gig and it was . . .

'A triumph!' Doris yelled, giving them all a cooling glass of lemon squash as their reward. 'You were amazing!' she said to everyone. 'Mrs Thickett, once you stood the right way, fantastic! Hector, great strumming on the guitar; maybe could do with a bit of polishing up? Hannah, what a gal, great backing singing. You could do with loosening up a bit but other than that perfect! And Ollie, what can I say? You were amazing!' Doris beamed. 'Now, fancy a little trip?'

'Where to?' Ollie asked, trying to catch his breath.

'Around the world!' she said, smiling.

LEAVING ON A JET PLANE

'A round the world!?' Ollie shrieked.

'Yes, I'm putting together a tour for you. We'll start with America . . .' Doris began.

'I'm in!' Hector yelled. He'd always wanted to go to America; it had been a lifelong dream, although it was mainly for the food. 'I want to go! Oh, imagine all those places to eat: KFC, Burger King, McDonald's.' Hector said dreamily.

'I know. It's such a shame you can't get any of that in this country.' Hannah shrugged.

'Are you serious?' Mum asked. 'You want us to

go round the world?'

'Yes. Look we need to take this show on the road—people want to see you. We could have sold this concert about ten times over,' Doris said.

'We're in!' Ollie yelled.

'Great, now it's time to get back to work,' Doris said. It seems that the work of being a pop star wasn't finished once you'd come offstage from performing. 'Time for some promo stuff,' Doris announced.

'What promo stuff?' Hannah asked.

'Oh, you know . . . the usual . . .' Doris grinned.

'Hello, we're The Twerpz and you are listening to KJP17 Radio in Japan. Konnichiwa!' Hector said into the microphone. 'How many more of these do I have to do?'

'How many are on the list?' Doris asked.

Hector looked at the list of radio stations he'd been given. He flicked the page over, then the next and then the one after that. 'HUNDREDS!' he yelled.

'Then do hundreds.' Doris shrugged.

They were still backstage at the Albert Hall, but

had moved to an area called the Green Room. It was the place where you stayed and relaxed before and after going onstage. Except it wasn't very relaxing. There seemed to be hundreds of people coming and going. Doris, fearful of being outed as the world's greatest record boss, had gone into disguise mode again as a big burly bodyguard called Dave. There were people delivering flowers, people carrying trays of food and drink, although exactly who they were for remained a mystery as Ollie, Hannah, Mum, and Hector certainly weren't getting any. They were too busy recording voice-overs for radio stations, or being pictured with fizzy drinks, or doing interviews for news channels about their incredible story from nobodies to superstars. There was even a rumour that the astronauts above planet earth had been watching, setting some sort of intergalactic record for viewing figures. Doris saw every second as an opportunity to promote either the world tour or get the band to promote a product; it all helped spread the word, strengthen the brand as it were.

Mum was talking to the nice gentleman from

CNN about how it was all going and what it was like being in the same band as your offspring, but she wasn't being very rock and roll about it. She'd taken it on herself to go into mum mode, and was passing round tea and bickies to the reporters as though they were neighbours who'd popped round for a gossip. Hannah was promoting some drink; it had all the flavour of sugar with none of the goodness of fruit, or was it the other way round? Anyway, she should have been, but she was busy on her phone. Hector was seemingly working through every radio station and bowl of sweets on earth saying how much he enjoyed listening to them when he was on tour in Japan, or Brazil, or wherever the radio station was from, which considering this was their first concert ever and the fact that Hector had never been anywhere further than

Clacton was clearly a lie; but that was the thing about show business, none of it seemed to matter.

'Can I have a word, Ollie?' Doris asked, beckoning Ollie towards a quiet corner of the room.

'Is everything alright?' Ollie asked, picking up Nigel and heading towards her.

'Yes, I'm going to go soon, too many people here, and I don't want to get spotted. Plus I'm at a really crucial stage of my knitting, but I just wanted to talk to you about the others.'

'Oh, okay,' Ollie said taken aback.

'You were great out there, a natural. The others were good too, but you looked at home. How did it feel?'

'The best!' Ollie beamed.

'Good. You know, I'm sure it'll all be alright . . .' Doris started.

'What will?' Ollie asked, not really sure where this chat was going.

'. . . you should just be aware, not many bands last forever. It's the way of things; things move on, people move on. With your band, who knows how long it'll last? Maybe a really long time. I really hope so, but the others . . .'

'What about them?'

'They . . . just don't seem to take it as seriously as you. It's like they're playing at it. Whereas you seem to really want it. You've got the hunger for it.'

'Oh . . .' Ollie said, looking around at the others. He looked at Hector's face deep in a bowl of what looked like Haribo—microphone abandoned. Mum was still circling the reporters with a plate of bickies, and Hannah continued to ignore the fact that she was supposed to be promoting a new fizzy drink as she chatted to her friends about how many free tickets she should get them to their next gig. Ollie looked down at Nigel in his carry case and then at Doris.

'I feel like the real talent is in this corner with me, and sometimes we have to make difficult decisions,' Doris said. 'Tonight you established yourself as the natural leader of this band. But, you need to ask yourself: are you, as the face of the band, pushing the others on and making them the best they can be, or are they holding you back? A band rarely lasts a long time, but a *solo* career on the other hand . . . well . . . just think about it.'

LET'S GET PHYSICAL

It was late by the time they got back to Big Records. Ollie and the rest of the Twerpz felt completely spent. Ollie couldn't help but think about what Doris had said to him about ditching the others. It made him feel awful; he couldn't do that. Everyone had worked so hard for the concert, and considering none of them were trained pop stars—if such a thing exists—they'd all done really well. Ollie made up his mind that he would tell Doris the idea about him going solo was a non-starter—yes, he was definitely going to do that the next time they had a moment alone.

'Good work today!' Doris said, leading the way. 'Tomorrow the training starts.'

'Training for what?' Hector asked.

'Training to be rock stars,' Doris said. Apparently such things do exist. 'To go on a world tour you have to be in good shape. We rise at 2 *a.m.*, we head down to the gym for pilloxing class—that's a mixture of pilates and boxing. It's incredible restful while being quite violent. After that it's a breakfast of green tea, egg whites and slapped avocados served on a piece of wood. Then at 4 *a.m.* we hit the isolation tanks hard for a forty-five minute intense aura cleansing and chi top-up. You then have a spin class, followed by a Japanese TV interview. Oh, I forgot to mention the intense Japanese language lesson at 3 *a.m.*' Doris beamed. 'After the interview we'll have a swim, run, and second spin class. It's like a triathlon, but a really quick one. Then it's rehydration time with a quick trip to the water restaurant—they're opening up for us early—then at 7 *a.m.* it's lunch.'

'We have lunch at seven in the morning?' Hannah

said, just exhausted listening to the words.

'This is your dream, Hector,' Mum added.

'Nightmare, you mean nightmare.'

'It's then two hours of school work.' Doris shrugged. 'I'm sorry, but those are the rules. That will take us to 9 *a.m.* After that we have another TV interview, with America; it's their *Late Late Late Show*. That's ten minutes. It's comedy, so please try and be hilarious,' Doris said, leading everyone out of the lift towards their suite. 'After that we have massages, followed by more school work. Then it's a couple of hours in the gym, followed by a marketing and branding meeting. We need to record some messages for foreign radio stations: "Bonjour, you're listening to Très Bien Radio . . ." that sort of thing, except it's for about four hundred radio stations. Then we have to go to the factory to launch your new range of pop star dolls. Then we hit the gym before the final lot of school work. Oh, but before that it's a solid five hours of rehearsal for the tour, followed by media training and a makeover,' Doris said, opening the door to their apartment. By now, The Twerpz were grey with fatigue. 'Welcome to being an international rock star. What did you think it would be, getting your photo taken and free stuff?' Doris asked.

'Well . . . yes, I did. We all did,' Hector answered. 'Wait, makeover? Does that mean that we get to ditch the superhero costumes?' Hector asked hopefully.

'Oh no, that's your signature look. We'll just, you know, add a bit of sparkle. Maybe a haircut too. Make-up, that sort of thing.'

'Look, I'm sure this pop star training sounds much worse than it is, but Doris is right, we need to be in good shape for this tour,' Ollie said, trying to be a peacemaker.

'Creep,' Hannah mouthed at him.

'But . . .' Ollie carried on, 'perhaps we could go a bit easy tomorrow, Doris? It has been a busy day,' Ollie pleaded. No matter what Doris had said about him going solo, he knew he wasn't ready for that; he needed his band behind him. For the meantime at least.

'Okay, okay . . . I'll tell you what, tomorrow we can go for a gentle workout, build up to the hard stuff.'

Doris smiled, realizing that she might be asking too much of the band, especially considering how many sweets, cakes, and pizzas Hector had polished off after the concert. 'Now get some rest, order anything you like; Big Records is paying for everything, for tomorrow is going to be the day that changes your life forever!' Doris beamed.

★

'WAKE UP!' Doris said, before blowing a whistle. 'EVERYONE GET OUT OF BED, INTO YOUR TRACKSUITS, AND MEET ME AT THE FRONT OF THE BUILDING IN FIVE MINUTES!' she yelled into a megaphone.

Moments later, The Twerpz were gathered outside the front of the building, yawning away, bed hair pointing in every direction and feeling very grumpy. 'Are we ready Twerpz?!' Doris yelled. She was dressed in a fluorescent pink tracksuit, and sat on an old-fashioned bicycle with a huge basket on the front.

'I thought we weren't going to do the full routine this morning!' Hector snapped. He was not a morning person at all.

'We're not, this is the gentle option. Basically, because we're running late, I've cleverly found a way to combine all of your new fitness and work regimes into one twenty minute workout. We're going to run to go get your makeovers, while doing school work, while your auras get cleansed, while eating eggs,' Doris announced proudly. 'Now, pop Nigel in the basket and we'll get going.'

'It's five-thirty in the morning!' Ollie whimpered.

'I know, you have had a very long lie-in, you should be very grateful,' Doris said, pulling a starter pistol out of her tracksuit pocket. 'Now on your marks, get set, go!'

BAAAAAAANG!

'ARGH!' everyone screamed with fear.

'COME ON! FOLLOW ON!' Doris screamed, while pedalling away at speed.

After a few tired glances, all the members began to jog after her.

'Please tell me the makcovers are happening in London and we're not jogging all the way to Paris or New York,' Hector sighed.

'What's the square root of fifty-six?' Doris asked, cycling away. 'Come on, answer correctly and I'll throw you an egg . . .'

An hour or so later, after a dicey bit when they went the wrong way round the bypass, they were in central London; tired, sweating, and picking egg and fish out of their hair.

'Sorry about getting lost. Still it was a nice bonus, that swim across the Thames,' Doris said, beaming.

There was a chorus of grunts and groans.

'Why couldn't I have sat in the basket like Nigel?' Hector panted.

'Because it's not a magic basket, Hector! You're too big! Never mind, we're here now.'

Hector, Ollie, Hannah, and Mum all looked up to see where they were. It was Harrods, the poshest department store in all of London.

'Time for a new image!' Doris announced, getting off her bike not a bit out of breath.

'I used to think Doris was a nice little old lady. Then I thought she was just a very determined business person. Now having spent more time with her, I've come to the conclusion she's a robot and we're now her slaves!' Hector gasped.

'I know what you mean. I guess she's a bit over the top, but it's all for the greater good. You could all show a bit more enthusiasm,' Ollie said.

'Listen, I'm all for a few new clothes and a haircut—anything that is frankly going to get me out of the Robin costume is a good thing—but it doesn't feel like *our* band anymore. It doesn't feel fun. Maybe you should have a word with her; she seems to listen to you,' Hector whispered as they walked through the big door into the department store towards a very excited-looking man who held out his arms and air-kissed Doris.

'What are you lot talking about?' Hannah and Mum asked, taking the opportunity to have a chat while Doris's back was turned.

'I'm trying to get Ollie to ask Doris to go easy on us. I know we signed a contract, but it feels like Doris owns us, and you know, I miss having fun. This doesn't seem much fun at the moment. Well, unless you're Nigel; she seems to have taken a real shine to him,' Hector added. 'So will you talk to her, Ollie?'

Ollie looked at Hannah and Hector and his Mum. Maybe Doris was right, why did the others not seem to be into this as much as him? 'Listen, I think Doris knows what she's doing,' Ollie said, pulling out a piece of paper from his pocket. 'Number two on the list of world domination is looking good. You can't argue with the list!' Ollie shrugged. 'We need to trust her. I mean she is buying us all new clothes and getting us haircuts and things.' He smiled. 'Give her a chance.'

'Attention please, Twerpz!' interrupted Doris. 'This is Salvatore. He's the best in the business. Salv, we need a new look for the band. We're off on tour and we need something striking, something original, something that's never been done before.'

'I know just the thing . . .' Salvatore grinned.

His white teeth flashed a big smile and he waggled his perfectly waxed eyebrows. '. . . GLITTER!' he announced.

'You see, that's not so bad,' Ollie said to Hector.

'I love it!' Doris clapped. 'And hair?'

'No hair at all!' He laughed.

'Perfect!' Doris said.

Hannah, Mum, and Hector all turned round and stared at Ollie.

14

BYE BYE BABY
(BABY GOODBYE)

'So, this is it. Goodbye, I guess. I don't know when I'll see you again. All I know is that I love you and I'll miss you. All I hope is that you remember me, and remember why I'm doing this; it's so that you'll have a good future. But this is the price we must pay my lovelies,' Hector whimpered.

'Oh, for goodness' sake, they're only a couple of gerbils. They won't even remember you when you've gone,' Ollie said, trying to chivvy Hector along.

'That's what I'm afraid of!' Hector sobbed.

'To be honest son,' Hector's mum said as she

held out the cage for Hector to prod, poke, and coo over, 'since your haircut, I don't think they know who you are. If anything they look a bit scared. I would too if I was their size and I saw that big dome coming towards me.'

'Look, Salvatore was the one who did it, which I still haven't forgiven him for, along with the rest of you. You all let me have my hair shaved off before chickening out yourselves. That's pretty shoddy behaviour in my eyes,' Hector said, narrowing his eyes.

'Look, I'm not going to let them shave my mother's head. That's simply not going to happen. Anyway, I don't know what you're complaining about, we all got a new look,' Ollie said.

'New look? You got some brand-new trainers, Hannah got a diamond-encrusted hoodie, and . . .'

'I got a brand-new blusher,' Mum said with a grin.

'It's hardly the same!' Hector sniffed.

'Oh, stop complaining, I bought you a hat didn't I?' Ollie said.

'It says: I lost my lunch at Chessington World of Adventure!' Hector growled.

'It's only until your hair grows back. I think your hat looks spiffing good,' Ollie muttered.

The band were at the airport, saying goodbye to their loved ones: family, friends, and gerbils. It was the beginning of what was going to be an epic world tour. They were playing all over the globe, zig-zagging continents, performing in tiny venues where their sound was stripped down, and large stadiums in front of huge crowds. It was still only the one song that they had. They were going to throw in a few cover versions to pad out the show, add a few videos in the background, a small laser display, and a couple of Doris's other acts were going to support them so fans had a fairly decent night out. Although it hadn't stopped people asking the question, what was going to be the next song? *Cat Attack* was still flying high in the charts; the downloads and views were off the scale. But in a world where the next big thing is just around the corner, Ollie was well aware that they needed a follow-up song, otherwise they might fall into the dreaded category of 'one-hit-wonder' and disappear into nothingness, never to be heard of or seen again. But all that was for another day; today they were off to start their tour.

'This way!' Doris said, pointing the way to a tiny jet parked on the runway. Like everything they'd travelled in lately, it had the band's logo all over it. The door popped open and revealed beautiful cream leather chairs, complete with personal TVs and a fridge packed with everything you might need to fly round the world.

The next few weeks were exhausting. The novelty of travel soon wore off. I mean, when you're in a band, all you really see is an airport, a coach or limo, the venue, then back to the airport to do the whole thing again. The band didn't get a day off, let alone an hour! This wasn't unusual; it was just the way things were when this was your job. It's endless. You never get a chance to sit back and enjoy the success. You know that it could all disappear at any second, so what do you do? You keep it going for as long as possible. Keeping the momentum up at all times. By the time the band landed in the last venue for the final concert of the tour, they were all frazzled.

'Hello . . . Cairo!' Hector boomed, coming on stage.

'Los Angeles!' Ollie corrected him.

'Whatever!' Hector yelled back. 'Let's have a party!'

Ollie tried to shrug it off, but this was typical of Hector; everyone else knew where they were, but Hector was always about three cities behind. When they were in Paris, he thought it was Blackpool.

When they were in Beijing, he thought it was Paris. And so on, and so on. At least this was the last show for a while. Doris, who had been around for some of the tour, was flying out for the last concert where she promised that they would have a couple of days' rest in the sun before it was back to the studio for more work. Ollie put all the tension behind him and decided to have a good show. It was their last for a while and he'd still had an amazing time on tour, even if it had dragged on a bit. The band finished up playing their song, said their goodbyes, and left the stage.

'Thank goodness for that!' Mum squawked. 'No offence dear, but if I have to hear that awful song one more time I may be forced to pull off my own ears.'

'Thanks mum,' Ollie snarked. 'Next time can we try and learn the name of the city?' Ollie asked, looking at Hector.

'Oh relax, don't be such a stick-in-the-mud!' Hector laughed. 'It always works out.'

'It always works out because we're all working hard to make it work out,' Ollie snapped. 'Well, except for Hannah—you were really phoning it in tonight. You need to put some effort in. We have spoken about this a few times now,' Ollie said, doing his best telling-off voice.

'Oh, shove it,' Hannah said.

'Oh well, that's charming isn't it? Mum, did you hear that?' asked Ollie.

'Mum did you hear that?' Hannah repeated under her breath in a funny voice.

'Wait, so let me get this right, *now* I'm the boss?' Mum snapped. 'I thought you were in charge of us all, Ollie, or is that only when you want me to take your side against Hannah?'

'Right, that's a twenty pound fine for insubordination in the ranks!' Ollie yelled.

'What does that mean?' Hector asked.

'It means when someone doesn't obey orders they have to pay up,' Hannah replied.

'Orders! Stop acting like you're in charge of us all, Ollie!' Hector shouted.

'Someone needs to take charge, and I'm the only one taking this job seriously. You thought America was Africa!' Ollie yelled.

'I'll tell you what, if you can spell insubordination, I'll cough up!' Mum boomed angrily.

'Hey guys!' Doris said, poking her head round the door and smiling. 'Who wants to get out of here?'

'I DO!' everyone yelled at once.

No one said a word to each other on the ride to the hotel. The sun was shining brightly, but the mood was glum. Was it him, or had they all been snapping at each other more and more lately, Ollie wondered. He was sure it was just tiredness; they had been at it non-stop since the upload had hit YouTube. It had gone from feeling like a dream to just feeling like a job. As the car pulled into the hotel all the bandmates went their own ways: Hector to the pool, swigging cherry pop and eating yet another bag of sweets; Mum to find a nice cup of tea; Hannah in search of the WiFi code so she could chat to her friends, who she complained that she missed all the time; and Ollie, well, it was left to him as usual to do any interviews, pose for selfies, and promote whatever radio station or TV channel needed promoting.

It was nearly midnight by the time Ollie had finished his commitments. He was on the garden terrace. It was quieter there, as there seemed to be some sort of hullabaloo happening inside the hotel. Security guards were being summoned and hotel staff were looking very angry.

'So how's it all been?' Doris said, having finally got rid of the last interviewer.

'Great!' Ollie said. He had Nigel with him who had been a real comfort these last few days. It was nice to have someone to talk to who didn't talk back. Ollie was painfully aware that Doris was sort of his boss, even though she made him call her Granny to throw people off the scent as to her real identity.

'Really?' she asked.

'Oh. *Really*? Well, if you want the real answer, no it's been awful. Hector is doing my head in, Hannah hates me, and no human should spend this amount of time with his mother without a pair of noise-cancelling earphones. You know, the sort that people digging the road use. I mean if you want the *real* answer!' Ollie sighed. 'I'm sorry; it's been a long few days. The shows have gone well, it's all gone well; it's just, you know, band stuff.'

'I know,' Doris said, nodding. 'Well, remember what I said before about going solo—' Doris didn't have time to finish her sentence before her phone started buzzing, as did Ollie's.

'TMZ Breaking News . . .' Doris read. 'Hector from the band The Twerpz is holed up in a LA hotel and has gone berserk!'

Ollie's phone read the same. They both looked at each other then up towards the penthouse suite where they could see something being thrown out of the window.

'Excuse me, Mr Ollie and Granny Ollie,' the hotel manager interrupted, 'we've been looking for you. There is huge problem with your friend!'

Doris and Ollie took one look at eachother and then immediately headed towards the lift. By now Doris could see TV trucks pulling up at the front of the hotel. 'That's the trouble these days, everyone has a phone,' Doris said, sprinting towards the closing door. 'If they have a phone, they're basically a TV Channel and reporter rolled into one. All it takes is one guest to see what's happening and you have a situation like this! What's he doing?' she asked the manager.

'He has locked himself into the penthouse suite and is throwing things out of the window because we refused to allow a group of fans to come back to his room and play Nintendo Switch,' the manager said, as the lift zoomed up to the top floor.

'He's also . . .' the manager said, '. . . consumed quite a lot of the mini bar.' His voice filled with shame at having to tell Ollie and Doris this information.

'How much?' Ollie asked.

'Three bottles of Cherryade, some Coca-Cola, and maybe three or four family bags of candy,' he said, shaking his head. 'And when we refused to bring him more, that's when he locked the room and started throwing things out of the window.'

The doors on the lift pinged open, and the three of them ran down to the corridor where hotel staff were busy trying to negotiate with Hector.

'I knew this would happen. I've been telling him to take it easy. Get water and bring fruit, as much fruit and soup as you can. We need to take the edge of this junk food high,' Ollie said.

'HECTOR!' Ollie shouted, banging on the door. 'LET ME IN!' There was a loud clattering of what sounded like the hotel being dismantled and thrown out of the window.

'THEY WON'T LET ME PLAY. ALL I WANT TO DO IS PLAY!' Hector yelled.

'Open up the door and we can play. Yeah, it'll be like old times, you and me bud,' Ollie pleaded. There was a pause for a second and then a smash of glass.

'Oh, for goodness' sake, stand back!' Doris cried out, before taking a step back and breaking down the door. All of them burst in to see Hector going—as the news report had stated—berserk! The bed was a mess where Hector had been jumping around. Hector had the TV in his hands and was charging to the window. It was too late to say anything; before Ollie could open his mouth, the TV was hurtling out of the window and into the swimming pool outside. Ollie watched it slap against the water before the whole thing sank to the bottom. They weren't the only witnesses; cameras from every TV station in town saw the whole thing too.

'YOU WANT TO PLAY WITH ME?' Hector whimpered, his eyes wild from the sugar binge. 'LIKE OLD TIMES?'

'Well, it's going to be harder now that the TV's in the pool,' replied Ollie. Just then, room service arrived with huge silver canteens of soups and fruit bowls.

'WHO'S THAT FOR?!' Hector wailed. 'WHAT ARE YOU DOING?' he cried as everyone grabbed some hot fresh wholesome soup and began surrounding Hector, like hunters trying to catch a wild beast.

'Now, it's going to be okay, just try some delicious vegetable broth,' Ollie coaxed, reassuringly. 'We're all here to help. We're your friends.'

THINGS CAN ONLY GET BETTER

'Hello, it's me Charlie James, voted Britain's Most Eligible Broadcaster 2001 by the readers of *Cardigan Wearers' Monthly*. I'm here with what some are calling the baddest rock band in the history of music. Others think it's all a gimmick, all a set-up, to disguise the fact that The Twerpz are a one-hit-wonder. But before all that, I think there's something that Hector, or "baldy Twerp" as some people have nicknamed him, has to say,' Charlie said, passing the microphone to Hector.

'Thanks,' Hector began, as he sat sternly on

his chair in the studio, wearing his extra glittery Robin costume and dark sunglasses. 'A few days ago, something happened to me. I had too much fizzy pop, too many sweets; I was riding high on a wave of adrenalin and Skittles.'

'Mostly Skittles I think,' Ollie added.

'Yep, yes it was, Ollie, thanks. To cut a long story short, I'd had a lot of bad things to eat and drink. I wasn't looking after myself. I wasn't having a balanced diet. I was surviving on a diet of sweet sugary garbage. And where did that take me? It took me to rock bottom. Where I now famously went berserk in a hotel. I have, of course, apologized to the hotel and to my bandmates.'

'Only one of whom is here today. Where are the others?' Charlie asked Ollie.

'Well, they are taking some time to rest. It's been a very busy few weeks, and what happened on that dark, dark night still affects us all. So to answer your question, Hannah has gone to a spa to recover, get some inner peace, and Mum has gone to an actual Spar to buy some eggs, bread, and milk and give dad his first home-cooked meal in weeks. That is, if she can entice him out of the shed where he has been living since we hit the big time. It's taken its toll on us all, Charlie; I won't lie to you.'

'Talk us through what happened that fateful night,' Charlie asked Hector.

'Well, I can talk you through what I remember. That isn't a lot to be honest. I know we'd finished a concert in Cairo was it? I think, somehow I ended up in LA,' Hector began.

Ollie sighed, putting his head in hands.

'Sorry, did you say something, Ollie?' asked Hector.

'Nope, you carry on.'

'I will, yes. I ended up in LA, and you know me, Charlie, I'm the fun one of the band; I just wanted to relax, you know. Sometimes you have to stop work and enjoy yourself, something that we could all learn to do better—'

'I relax,' Ollie interrupted, 'but I just have to do more work than you. I mean, I am the sort of leader of the band. I'm the boss of the collective.'

'A collective doesn't have a boss,' Hector said, trying not to lose his temper. 'Anyway, all I wanted to do was play video games with a few of the fans, and that's when things started to go wrong. The hotel staff didn't seem to like this idea, or the fact that I wanted more cherry pop. That's when the sweets kicked in and I became disruptive . . . apparently. I say apparently because I don't remember. It's a blur.'

'Hector throws TV out of window,' Charlie read aloud, showing Hector the paper. 'I think we have footage of you throwing a trouser press into the swimming pool and cushions too,' Charlie said, playing a clip from his tablet.

'Yes, fortunately, all the TV stations and papers were there to remind me of the whole evening. I do remember getting very cross about the amount of cushions on the hotel bed. There seemed to be so many cushions, and in my state, it made no sense to me.'

'And that's why you're fronting a new healthy eating campaign isn't it?' Charlie asked.

'Absolutely. It's called "Just Say Veg". It's about turning your back on the damage that too much pop can have and saying yes to fruit and vegetables. I've been clean for nearly three weeks now; not one sweet, or glass of Cherryade has passed my lips.'

'And how's it been?' Charlie asked.

'So boring, I can't tell you,' Hector replied.

'So you're well on the road to recovery, Hector, and the band has taken a break. I guess the big question is: what's next for The Twerpz? I mean the last few weeks have been quite bad for you guys, and now I hear you're off to record some new songs; or rather I should say another song. How does it feel Ollie, Hector, that for the first time in a while you're going to be locked in a room together writing again? Are you confident you can recreate another hit like last time? Are you excited?'

Hector and Ollie looked at each other, gulped and then smiled their biggest fake smile.

'We simply can't wait,' Ollie beamed.

HIT ME BABY
ONE MORE TIME

'Hello Mum,' Ollie said nervously.

'Hello, son,' Mum said tersely.

'Hello everyone,' Ollie said with a nod. It was the first time the band had been back in the room since Hector had gone berserk. The room in question was the main studio at Big Records. All the greats had recorded there: The Beatles, The Stones, both Rolling and Roses, The Who, Hendrix, Gaga, Jay-Z, and The Wurzels. The place was a Mecca for any musician worth their salt. A place that oozed with creative genius and glowed with gold and platinum discs.

Ollie was the first to arrive. He had Nigel with him, in a gold carry case. The studio was all set up with the band's instruments and microphones; anything and everything a band could need to make a hit. Except of course the band had no actual songs, or even ideas for songs. There was an awkward silence as everyone else began to arrive. They all looked at each other and said nothing. Things had been very frosty at home, with Ollie, Mum, and Hannah only seeing each other at mealtimes, and when they did, there was lots of sighing and tutting whenever someone asked for the salt to be passed. Ollie had rehearsed this moment, the moment when they would all have to work together again, over and over in his head so many times, but he'd never got past 'Hello' in his mind.

'Hello dearies!' Doris said as she poked her head behind the door in her usual cheery way.

'DORIS!' everyone yelled with delight. The prospect of someone else being in the room suddenly lifted everyone's spirits; the awkwardness just seemed to evaporate.

'LOOK EVERYONE! DORIS IS HERE! COME IN. STAY. STAY FOR AGES! PLEASE. . .!' Ollie begged.

'Is everyone alright?' She looked around the room, sensing the tension. 'Oh I see, second album syndrome,' she said. 'Well, in your case, second song syndrome.'

'What's that?' Hector said, chomping on an apple.

'It happens to everyone. A band makes a brilliant first album, and then they have to follow it up. Bands worry that they can't do it again. That's what you're going through. How do you write the next song? How do you keep it fresh, original, yet familiar, when you're all probably sick of the sight of each other?'

'Yes, YES!' Ollie cheered. 'How *do* we do all those things?!'

Doris shrugged. 'I'm not a musician; I'm just the woman in charge of the machine. I do my job, bands do theirs. You'll figure it out. The best thing you can do is lock yourselves into the studio and recreate the magic. Just try and make the next song different.'

'Different, right,' Hannah repeated, nodding.

'The world doesn't want to hear the same song again,' Doris said.

'Okay, okay, we can do that,' Hector agreed.

'Of course,' Doris added, 'don't make it too different. It needs to be the same so it sounds like you.'

'Rightio . . . So the same and yet different?' Ollie nodded.

'But it needs to be new, yet familiar,' Doris added.

'Okay, so different as well as the same, new but also familiar,' Ollie clarified. 'That's very helpful.'

'Oh, good news, I've booked us a prime spot on the National Talent Gala, for the new single. Everyone will be watching, and the most influential celebrities will be in the audience, so you'd better write a good one. Right now dears, I have to go. Lady Gaga's having a rough time on her new album and locked herself in her studio and won't come out. You see, it doesn't get any easier!' Doris chuckled. 'Byyyeeeeeee.'

There was a loud clank as the door shut and

then more silence. After a second or two, Ollie broke the ice. 'Listen, I think we have all learnt a valuable lesson about life these last few weeks. I say we try to put all this behind us and get on with it. All we need to do is write a hit song. Let's just do that and we can be friends again.'

'Erm . . . okay . . .' Hector agreed, 'but are you going to be, you know, nice to us?'

'I'm always nice!' Ollie said, smiling. 'Aren't I?!'

Everyone looked down at their feet. 'You can be a bit shouty,' Mum muttered.

'Look, someone has to be the boss. I don't mean boss, but you know, the leader—NO! Not leader! Look, someone has to drive the bus; I'm just the friendly bus driver. Yeah, that's right, a nice old friendly bus driver in a hat.'

Hector looked confused and turned to Hannah.

'It's a metaphor, Hector. There is no bus. It's just another way for Ollie to call himself the boss.' Hannah shook her head. 'The trouble is, how can we write a song?' she asked. 'I mean, we can't ask Nigel.' Everyone looked over at Nigel, who had decided the whole thing was too tiring and gone to sleep. 'Last time we tried to get him to write a song, he went berserk in the room and trashed the place—sorry, Hector that was insensitive of me. I wasn't comparing you to a cat, or making light of your . . . plight,' Hannah said, trying to find the words.

'That's okay. It's all about owning your problems. I'm fine. Honesty is a good thing. My fruitist has taught me that.'

'What's a fruitist?' Ollie asked.

'A fruit adviser and spiritual healer.'

'Your what?' Mum asked, looking confused.

'He helps me,' Hector said calmly.

'You just need to stop drinking seven bottles of fizzy pop and eating five bags of sweets in one go. How much are you paying your fruitist?' Mum asked. 'You can have that one for free!'

'I think we're getting off topic. The song? Does anyone have any ideas?' Ollie asked. There was silence. 'Okay, in that case, back to plan A.'

★

Ten minutes later and Nigel was still refusing to come out of his cage. 'Come on, Nigel. Do you want to come

out and write a really cool song?' Ollie said, trying to coax the sleepy cat out of its slumber. 'Please? I'll give you loads of money.'

'I can always dress as a dog again?' Hector suggested.

'NO!' everyone snapped.

'We can't keep destroying stuff. We need to be clever,' Ollie added. 'Come on, Nige,' he repeated, using his best cutesy voice. 'Oh, it's no good; it's almost as if he doesn't understand me.' Ollie sighed.

'What about if we hold the cage over the keyboard and give it a shake until he pops out?' Hector said. 'He'll land on the keyboard, and at least he'll make a tune.'

'Do you mean throw the cat at the piano?' Hannah clarified.

'No, not throw, more like let gravity do its work.' Hector shrugged.

'We could smear the piano in cat food. I'd bet he'd go for that,' Mum suggested.

'I don't think smearing anything over this very expensive equipment is going to help,' Ollie said.

'Right, there's nothing else to do but do it ourselves. If the cat won't write us a song, I guess we'll have to do it.' Ollie shrugged. 'Frankly this is shoddy behaviour, Nigel, very shoddy.'

Ollie stood in front of his keyboard. Hector picked up the guitar and recorder. Mum stood with her maracas, and Hannah just stood there. 'What do I do?' she asked. 'I mean, I am the only person here who's had piano lessons, so maybe I should have a keyboard?'

'Erm, no,' Ollie said, looking around. 'There's only one, so why don't you stand there and just be quiet,' Ollie said, taking charge.

'What?' Hannah snorted. 'Just stand there and—'

'Be quiet!' Ollie said. 'You're being very distracting. Stand there,' he said, pointing to a specific bit of the floor. 'No, not there, you're in my eyeline. I can't create if people are in my eyeline. Just move back. No, further!'

'I'll tell you what, why don't I just stand out there?' Hannah said, pointing at the exit.

'Whatever!' Ollie said, adjusting the setting on

his keyboard so furiously that he didn't even notice Hannah storm out.

Mum took a tiny step back so she wasn't in Ollie's eyeline either. Then another. Then another.

'MOTHER! Stop shaking your maracas!' Ollie snapped. 'All I ever hear from you is maracas!'

'Well, I am the maraca player!' Mum yelled before throwing them down and following Hannah out of the studio.

Hector looked at his watch. 'Twenty-three minutes and thirty-nine seconds. That's how long it's taken to lose fifty per cent of the humans in the band. That's pretty impressive.'

'What? Oh, they'll be back. We're the talented ones anyway,' Ollie said, pointing at the three of them.

'You've just called the cat more talented than your own mother and sister. Hannah is very talented. I mean, she's great at so many things—' Hector sighed.

'Right, can we please stop talking about this? Can you leave Hannah out of it? I mean, what can I say man; it's time to choose sides between her and me. Maybe it's time I reconsidered our writing

184

partnership. Doris says—'

'Go on, what does Doris say?' Hector said, throwing down his guitar and recorder.

'Look, all I mean is there have been talks, ideas, whisperings of a solo career, and so far I've been very good; I haven't said yes.'

'A solo career for you?!' Hector yelled out in shock.

'I was going to talk to Doris. She wants me to go solo, you know, as I'm the leader, the talented one. But I thought if I asked her really nicely, she'd keep you on too. You know, as a favour to you?'

'A favour!'

'Yes, a favour, you know, as you're a friend. The crowd loves you; me up there being cool, you standing at the side, being . . . funny.'

'The funny one!' Hector shrieked with outrage. 'Let me get this straight; you'd keep me on to have something to laugh at?'

'No promises, but yes! You said yourself you bring the LOLs,' Ollie said, grinning.

'I quit!' Hector yelled. 'Oh, and I only went along

with all this to be close to Hannah. And as for the talented one, let me just work out the song-writing tally in my head. Oh yes, it's Ollie, ZERO, Nigel the bottom-licker, ONE! You're not the friend I thought you were. I don't know who you are any more. You go solo. I wouldn't want to hold you back!'

ALL BY MYSELF

TWANGGGGGG!

BOOOoooooOOOoooooOOOoooooik!

TWAAAAACCCCK!

BRRRRUMBRRRRRMMM PLINK PLONK!

CLAAAAAAAAAAAANK! were just some of
the many strange sounds that came out of Studio
A at the top of Big Records. It had been five days
since Hector, Hannah, and Mum had all stormed
out of the recording studio, and Ollie had had a

solo career thrust upon him. Even Nigel wandered off a few hours later. Ever since then, he'd been on a songwriting binge, a five-day musical lock-in, in which Ollie had embarked on a journey to reinvent music again. Instruments had been ordered, sent in, and used. No one had seen Ollie for days; all he did was eat and drink occasionally, nip to the loo, and play music. It was difficult to work out how it was going as the studio was mostly soundproof. All that leaked out were occasional loud thunderings and odd twangs. What Ollie was doing, or what he was making, was a mystery.

'How's it going in there?' Doris asked one of the many assistants who worked at Big Records.

THRRRRRRUUUUUUNK!

'Not sure. I don't think it's going well.'

'Hmm.' Doris knocked on the door. The dim and distant clattering stopped for a second. 'Hi Ollie, it's Doris. Do you want a mint? I just wondered how it was going. You see we have the concert in a couple of days, and well, I thought it might be a good idea

188

to actually let someone else hear the song? I think if we take it to the others—Hector, Hannah, and your Mum—you know, say you're sorry—we might all be able to play the National Talent Gala. I mean, your fans are expecting all of you. I suppose we could tell them that the others are ill or something.'

The door opened a crack. 'You were the one who suggested I go solo.'

'Suggested, is the word dearie, and I didn't mean quite so soon.'

'Well, I'm not solo anyway. Come in and see. It's going great!' Ollie smiled, a wild smile—the smile of a person who's been locked away in a room with nothing but instruments for too long.

Doris opened the door. 'Oh my!' she gasped.

'These are my new bandmates!' Ollie said, pointing at the studio. 'This is Mr Guitary, and this is Mr Bongos.'

'Ollie dear, that's a guitar with a big painted face on it. And those are some drums wearing a hat.'

'They're my new bandmates. This is Mike!' Ollie said, pointing at a mic stand with a wig on. 'Do you want to hear my song? It came to me in a dream!' Ollie laughed weirdly.

'Okay . . .' Doris nodded.

Ollie hit the drum button on his keyboard. And began to nod his head rhythmically.

PLONK PLONK PLONK PLONK PLONK PLOOOOONK PLONK.

He began to play. 'Do you like it? It's so familiar. It's like it wrote itself!' Ollie laughed.

'Yes, there's a reason for that!' Doris said, hitting the off button on the keyboard.

'What?' Ollie said, looking confused.

'It's *Baa Baa Black Sheep*. You've written a song that's already been written.'

'No, it's not!' Ollie began to play it again. 'You see? It's completely diff—oh no, it is *Baa Baa Black Sheep*,' he finally agreed. 'Oh, but Mr Bongos loved it.' Ollie sighed, visibly deflating like a balloon in front of Doris.

'You mean the drum kit with a hat on top?'

'Oh, well, in this light maybe,' Ollie said as if waking up from a terrible dream. 'I think I might need to go home, maybe get some rest.' He looked defeated. 'I don't think I'm very good at this.' He sighed and looked around the room, wondering quite what had happened in his life that his friends and family had all disappeared, and his only pals in the world were musical instruments in human headgear. 'I don't feel so good. I think . . . I think . . . I miss everyone,' he said softly.

'Why don't I call your Mum?' Doris said with a kindly smile.

Ollie sat in the foyer of Big Records, feeling sad, embarrassed, and lonely. Like a sick kid waiting to be picked up from the nurse's office. Just at that very second, Mum popped her head round the door. Ollie couldn't help but grin. It doesn't matter how famous you are, or how silly you've been, everyone needs their mum from time to time.

'Hi,' Ollie said.

'Doris phoned, said you weren't very well?' Mum said calmly.

'Actually, what she said was that you'd gone a bit bonkers in the nut and were talking to drum kits. I thought I'd tag along for a laugh,' Hannah said coming into the room too.

'Oh Mum,' Ollie sighed. 'What have I done? I was so mean to all of you. I thought I knew better than everyone. And what did I write? What was my great song? *Baa Baa Black sheep*, played really quite badly. I don't think I'm actually musical you know,'

192

he said in a moment of realization.

'Well, of course you're not,' Hannah guffawed. 'Music is something that you actually have to learn. It's not something you can get right first time. That's why there are music teachers. If everyone could do it, then everyone would be doing it.'

'What are we going to do? We're supposed to be debuting our single tomorrow,' Ollie groaned. 'I wish none of this had happened. I wish Nigel hadn't remixed our song. I wish I hadn't lied. I wish I could turn the clock back—wait, that's it!' Ollie yelled. 'Doris, where's Doris?'

'Yes poppet?' Doris said, looking up from her desk at the sight and sound of Ollie bursting into her office.

'Don't cancel the gig. I know what to do! I know what to play!'

'Er . . . are you sure?' Doris said.

'YES! Tell the press; tell the world, it's a HUGE exclusive!' Ollie grinned.

'Okay . . .' Doris said, looking confused.

'Erm, Ollie, what's the plan? Please tell me there's

a plan?!' Hannah asked.

'Oh, there's a plan, Hannah. Pass me my keyboard. Doris, can we borrow a limo? It's time to get the band back together!'

SORRY SEEMS TO BE THE HARDEST WORD

Ollie took a deep breath and stood alone at his keyboard. He cleared his throat and prepared himself for the most important gig of his life.

'HEeeeeEEEEEeeeector . . .' he sang. 'I'm really sorry I was a twerp. Being a twerp didn't work. Beeeeeeing ace is reallllllly rather great!' Ollie sang underneath Hector's bedroom window.

There was a twitch of a curtain and a jolt as the window was hooked open. Hector stood open-mouthed for a second, trying to work out what was going on, along with Nigel who had leapt up onto the windowsill to get a look at what was happening. 'You know, it's more effective if you actually plug the keyboard in?' Hector yelled out of the window to Ollie.

'I know. I couldn't find the big extension lead. I think Dad's still got it for power-hosing emergencies. Nige! That's where you went!'

'What are you doing?' Hector cried out.

'I'm trying to say sorry. Except it's really hard to think of anything that rhymes with sorry.'

'Lolly, brolly, trolley, lorry, folly—there's literally loads of things that rhyme with sorry,' Hector bellowed down into the street.

'This is why I need you back in the band. I need your songwriting brilliance. I'm soooooo sorry. I was off my trolley to be mad at you. Here have a lolly. It's fresh from the lorry—'

'Please stop singing!' Hector cried out. 'I'll come back, but on one condition!'

'Erm, okay, what?' Ollie asked nervously. Was it more royalties? Image rights?

'Just don't be a wally,' Hector said.

'Oh, yeah, okay. Hey, wally rhymes too!' Ollie laughed.

'No, it doesn't,' Hannah sighed as she and Mum witnessed the whole thing from the pavement. 'In fact, neither does lolly. You two are really bad at writing songs,' she said, shaking her head.

'Oh, who cares?! He's back. My boy is back!' Ollie cheered.

A few minutes later, the limo was zooming to the Theatre Royal, the venue for tonight's National Talent Gala performance. In the back were Mum, Hector, and Hannah, all staring at Ollie wondering what the big plan was.

'Soooooo?' Hannah asked. 'I presume you have an idea?'

'Yes!' Ollie said, looking at everyone. 'The song we're going to do tonight, the new song is—'

'Yes?!' everyone asked eagerly.

'The old song!' Ollie said triumphantly.

'What?' Mum, Hannah, and Hector asked.

'Let me explain,' Ollie continued. 'Do you remember that afternoon in my bedroom, Hector? Remember what we were playing before Nigel came in?' Ollie asked.

'Yes, I was strumming a C chord. I remember because I only know two other chords,' Hector said.

'You played; I put the drumbeat on the keyboard. I think you tooted an F on the recorder.'

'I remember. And then Nigel came in and discoed it up,' Hector said, nodding.

'Well, let's play the original. And the best thing about it is that it's our song!'

'But it's completely different to the one that got uploaded, the one the world knows you for,' Hannah said. 'I heard it.'

'I don't care; it's ours. At least now we can stop pretending, stop lying, and be ourselves. All this deceit has been driving us apart. Finally we can be the band that we were meant to be.'

'But what if the world doesn't like who you are?' Mum asked.

'Well, then I don't care. I've spent so long trying to be what everyone else wants, and it's exhausting. I haven't had time to enjoy the fame because I've been too busy trying to keep up with a massive lie. What's the point in pretending if you don't have time to have fun any more? If you're always snapping at your best friend and trying to coax a cat into writing songs? If the world doesn't like me, fine. I know that I will have done the right thing. Will you guys help me?' Ollie asked.

Hannah, Mum, and Hector all grinned and nodded.

'Hurrah! Now all we need to do is tell Doris,' Ollie said nervously.

'Agh, just in time!' Hector said, looking out of the car window. 'There she is now!'

The car pulled up at the theatre. It was still a few hours before the National Talent Gala performance, but it was already abuzz with activity. Doris had done her part by proclaiming to the world that tonight's performance would be some kind of exclusive announcement; she just didn't know what it was. There at the stage door was a nervous looking Doris.

'I should be in full costume; I might be spotted!' she said in a tailspin. 'Can someone explain to me what's going on?'

'Yes!' said Ollie as he got out of the car with a spring in his step for what seemed like the first time in ages. 'I am—'

'Yes?' Doris said. 'Yeees?'

'Going un-solo!'

'What?'

'I am de-solo-ing myself from myself!' Ollie tried again.

'You're doing what now?' Doris asked.

'The solo-ing, that I'd planned to do on my own, has been undone, and thus I will be uncoupling myself, from me with immediate notice,' Ollie clarified.

'Are you ill?'

'NO! I have never been weller!' Ollie beamed.

'He means the band's back together.' Hannah shrugged.

'Ohhhh, great!' Doris said. 'So, the concert, the new song, the one that you had a week to write, the one that turned out to be *Baa Baa Black Sheep* . . .?'

'What?' Hector asked, trying to catch up.

'Don't worry. I was talking to the drums back at the studio. It was all very weird, but I'm fine now,'

Ollie said reassuringly. 'But *Baa Baa Black Sheep*'s gone, and we have a new song,' he continued. 'It's one we wrote ages ago.'

'Well, you best go and rehearse it!' Doris said, looking at the time. Just then her phone rang. 'Yes? He's done *what*?' she shrieked. 'Okay,' she sighed, ending the call. 'I have to go, Mick Jagger's having a crisis . . .' She picked up her phone and dialled 999. 'Hello? Is that the fire brigade?' she asked. She turned to Ollie. 'I'll see you later for the show. I'm sure your new song will be a hit, and if it's not, I'll just fire you!' she said hopping into the limo.

The remaining hours were spent polishing the song. Hannah took over the keyboards, and began to add even more layers of music. Hector went on YouTube and learnt another three chords so that he actually sounded like a guitarist. Mum turned out to be a whizz on the drums and 'slapped a funky dub-step beat all over the jam' to use her words. And what started out as an idea—and here's the amazing thing—actually sounded a bit like a song. Ollie had worked on his lyrics so they actually made sense.

He threw in a few verbs to go with his collection of romantic nouns until they had something that they could be proud of. Incredible things happen when you stop being a collection of individuals and start working as a team. Ollie was happy. They were all happy. Even Nigel was happy. Well, truth be told, Nigel was asleep, which meant that he was quiet and not violent, which made everyone else happy. By the time the rehearsal had finished it was almost time for the concert. The question was, what would Doris and the public make of The Twerpz' new sound? There was only one way to find out.

'Two minutes to go!' a burly assistant said, poking his head into the dressing room.

'Oh, come on Doris. You'll have to do better than that,' Hector said, trying to pull the skin off the big man's face. 'Arggghhhh! I think you've used too much glue Doris. It's like it's your real face,' Hector said, struggling to get a grip on the man's head.

'Hector, what are you doing?' Doris said, walking into the dressing room. 'Hello, I'm just an innocent granny, that's all,' she said to the poor man who was having his face pulled off. 'Hector! Stop it!' she snapped.

'Oops, sorry,' Hector said, rearranging the poor chap's features so that they all looked normal again.

'Two minutes!' the guy repeated, storming off.

'How did the sound check go?' Doris asked. 'What's the new song like? The same but different?'

'I don't know about that, but it's us. We have our sound. It is what it is.' Ollie shrugged.

Suddenly the bell rang to signal it was time for people to take their seats. It was time for the National Talent Gala to start. It was the most showbiz night of the year, where all the top stars would perform in front of an A-list audience. All the greats had done it. It was a night so prestigious that it could propel you into super stardom or finish you there and then. The dressing room cleared out and it was just the band. They all looked at each other. It felt so good to be friends again.

'Are we ready?' Ollie asked.

'Yes,' everyone said. Everyone except Hector.

'No, no,' he said.

'Not now Hector, I said I was sorry. I meant it. You can't leave me now. You can't take off your leggings. Why are you taking off your leggings?' Ollie asked in horror.

'Something feels wrong. Listen; if we're going to be ourselves, we need to *be* ourselves. No more costumes, no more masks. Let's just be us!'

Ollie smiled. Hector was right. It was time to ditch the disguises and just be normal. 'Oh my, that feels so goooooooood!' Ollie yelled as he peeled the costume off. Fortunately, he hadn't gone commando and was wearing trousers, T-shirt, the full works.

'Well, I'm not ditching my hat!' Mum said. 'I paid nearly thirty pounds for this. I don't care about honesty and all that; I want my money's worth!'

'Time to gooooo!' the stage manager yelled, coming back into the room. 'Wait, who are you?'

'I'm a Twerp!' Ollie said. 'Now, let's rock this joint!'

A NIGHT AT THE OPERA

'Hello Londooooooon!' Ollie yelled, walking out onto the stage. There was silence as everyone looked confused. Who were these people? They *sounded* like The Twerpz, but I mean, they were wearing normal clothes. Where was the glitz? Where was the sparkle? Mum took her place on the drums, to gasps of horror. No maracas shaking? Hannah on keys instead of backing vocals? This was madness. Hector tuning his guitar like he knew more than three chords—incredible!

'I'd like to take a second to talk to you all,' Ollie

said as he walked to the microphone.

Doris stood at the side of the stage, back in her disguise, scarcely able to work out what was going on.

'Our song, our worldwide hit, *Cat Attack* was a lie. We didn't write it.'

There were huge gasps from everyone.

'It's time you knew the truth . . .' Ollie paused. 'Nigel the cat wrote that song! Many of you will have seen him. He's been like a mascot for us: one that has travelled around the world with us. And now you know why,' he announced dramatically. There were cries of disbelief all around, from Doris as well as all the people watching at home. 'I know. I know. He went a bit crazy, danced all over the keyboard and remixed the song that became *Cat Attack*. So here's the truth. The song that we actually wrote is the one we're about to play you. It's called,

Baby, I Love You Baby. Now I know that you've been lied to, and that's my fault. Instead of owning up and telling everyone that Nigel was the creative force behind *Cat Attack*, I went along with it all. I was desperate for fame, so I fed the lie. It nearly destroyed me, my family, and my friends. And for that I'm sorry. So with your permission, we'd like to sing you our real song, the song that we actually wrote; one that comes from the heart. Because sometimes it's not about the mistakes you make, it's about how you fix them. I am, after all, a boy standing in front of his fans, asking them to listen to a song that I wrote and that a cat didn't.

'So I hope you don't mind, but here it goes, it's called *Baby, I Love You Baby*—for clarification, it's not about babies, it's about, you know, kissing and love and all that sort of stuff that sells records, I mean, that's not what why we wrote it, well, not entirely . . . you know, I think there's such a thing as too much honesty . . . okay people let's do this.' Ollie signaled to the other members of the band to get ready. Then, he gulped away his nerves and began to play, tentatively at first, but by the time the drums kicked in and Hector started playing those chords on his guitar, Ollie was performing like a true rock star—crooning, 'Baby, I Love You Baby' into the mic with all his heart. Maybe it was the fact that Ollie felt like he was being his true self for the first time in years, or maybe it was the fact that he'd bared his soul to an audience of millions, but the performance was his best yet.

Ollie had never felt more in tune with the world, with his sound, with music itself. And it was like everyone else on stage was experiencing the same thing: Mum was totally in the groove on drums, Hector hadn't missed a single chord on guitar, and Hannah was an absolute wizard on the keys—they were really doing it, everything was going perfectly, they were rock stars.

Before Ollie knew it, he was out of lyrics, it had felt like only seconds and now the whole experience was over. The song had been given to the audience, a musical hug for the ears. All those *Cat Attack* lies seem to melt away. This is what people really want, they don't want gimmicks, they want the truth. They want honesty, they want *Baby, I Love you Baby*.

'Thank you,' Ollie graciously said into the mic. 'Thanks to each and every one of you.'

There was a moment of absolute silence, followed by a few mutterings, and then applause rumbling round the theatre, before finally a chant of approval began to echo around the place. Ollie looked at the others and grinned.

'Nigel . . .
Nigel . . .
NIGEL!' the crowd began to cheer, louder and louder. The smile disappeared from Ollie's face. 'Seriously? After all that? You want—'

'NIGEL!' the crowd boomed.

'It's a world gone mad!' Ollie yelled above the noise from the crowd. 'Come on, let's get out of here!'

⭐

'If this lot docsn't want to hear our song, I'll find someone who does.' Ollie said, back in the dressing room.

'THE CAT WROTE THE SONG!'

Doris screamed, storming into the room.

'THE CAT WROTE THE SONG!'

she roared.

'Yes, kind of,' Hector sighed, nibbling on a clementine. 'I wish I had some chocolate,' he whined.

'Are you mad?!' Doris continued yelling.

'Look, who's madder? Us, or the people who actually bought the song, downloaded it, and came to the concert?' Ollie said, defending himself. 'They thought a song by a cat was good! It's not; it was an awful song, Doris! Terrible! One of the worst ever written!'

'I know that! I do have ears!' Doris cried out.

'Wait, what, you hated the song too?' Mum asked.

'Yes, everyone did, that's why people loved it so much. They loved it because it was terrible. It was the Sharknado of music.'

'Sharknado?' Hannah asked.

'A film so bad, it's good. It's about a tornado full of sharks,' Hector helpfully pointed out.

'I guess this means we're fired?' Ollie asked nervously.

'Yes, yes it does. You signed a contract to say that you were the songwriter; that's not worth the paper it's written on now.'

'So that's it? It's over?' Mum asked, looking upset.

'The world knows now,' Doris sighed. 'If you'd told me about it sooner, maybe something could have been done. But my contract is with the creators of *Cat Attack*.'

'What does that mean?' Hannah asked.

Everyone looked over at Nigel who had been napping as usual through the important bit. Slowly but surely he woke up and when he saw Doris, leapt up into her arms.

'Oh, I see. Thanks for the loyalty, Nigel,' Ollie sniffed.

'Thanks for the ride kids, and if you ever write anything as bad as *Cat Attack*, drop me a line, but until then . . .' Doris smiled.

'What?' Ollie asked.

⭐

'. . . Nigel, let's talk about the second single. Do you have a passport? I could get you on the *Tonight* show by the end of the week. I'm thinking a photo shoot, makeover . . .' Doris said, carrying Nigel with her. She picked up her phone. 'Hello? Is that Salvatore?'

BACK FOR GOOD

SIX MONTHS LATER . . .

'Hello, and welcome to another episode of *Where Are They Now?* with me, handsome and award-winning broadcaster, Charlie James. TONIGHT—'there was the sudden sound of dramatic drums and serious trumpets as the theme tune kicked in—'. . . I talk to the biggest, arguably most controversial band in the history of music. They granted me exclusive access to their comeback gig. It's a story of success, fame, and friendship. How they went from nobodies to the most famous musical act in the world. And how it all came crashing down on that fateful night at the National Talent Gala. What became of the band? Where are they now? Viewers should be aware that some scenes may feature bright flashing images, mostly when I flash my perfect and very white teeth. I'm sorry, but there's nothing I can do about that,' said Charlie, flashing a bright white grin. 'NOW, LET'S GOOOOOOO!'

The rest of the theme tuned played; there were lots of dramatic shots of Charlie James running after people with his camera, like he was a journalistic superhero tracking down celebrities of years gone past. As the show played out across the country, the streets seemed a little quieter across Britain. Maybe it was a coincidence, or maybe it's because everyone had snuck home early to find out the next chapter of this extraordinary story: how two friends became the biggest, brightest stars in the world, and how they lost it all.

'So guys, I wonder if you could tell us how it all began for you. Was music always a big part of your life?' Charlie asked, holding out a microphone in front of two twelve-year-old boys. Ollie was swigging from a fizzy pop bottle as he sat with a huge mirror behind him, surrounded by flowers and cards from well-wishers. Sat next to him surrounded by every type of fruit imaginable was his best friend, Hector.

'Well Charlie, music was definitely where it started. We always loved music, and we had a feeling it was our ticket to the big time. You may have called us dreamers.' Ollie smiled. 'I guess that this gig is about, you know, getting back together after all that was said and done, trying to write the perfect ending to a crazy dream.'

'That's absolutely right, Ollie. It always felt like we had unfinished business,' Hector agreed.

'And have you two made up? I know that things haven't always been easy,' Charlie asked.

'Yeah . . .' Ollie and Hector both replied.

'We're all good,' Ollie said, taking over the conversation. 'For me this has always been about other people—that connection—whether that's with strangers or friends. There is no 'I' in music after all, Charlie.'

'Well yeah, there is,' Hector replied.

'Well, obviously there is an 'i' in it. What I mean is that I like to think of it as a gift for others, like a really good gift, you know? Not like a book token or some bubble bath, but a really good one, like a dolphin. I like to think about the dolphins when I make music; I just really want to save the dolphins I guess.'

'Is there a shortage of dolphins?' Hector asked.

'Can you have too many dolphins?' Ollie replied.

'Yes, too many dolphins would be a nightmare. Imagine if you were trying to walk down the street but you had to keep stepping over dolphins all the time.'

'What about you, Hector? Do you make music for the animals?' Charlie asked, a tad confused.

'I make music for the fans,' Hector replied. 'They're the ones who buy, or rather bought our music. I mean, I don't think a dolphin has ever bought any of our stuff?'

'Are you making fun of me?' Ollie asked. 'Do you not care about the elephants and the dolphins?'

'Elephants now, is it? Yes, I care about all the animals, but I just care about the fans more,' Hector snapped.

'So anyway,' Charlie tried to interrupt.

'Are you saying I don't care about the fans?' Ollie asked indignantly.

'I'm not saying anything,' Hector shrugged.

'Oh, you seem to be saying quite a lot! This is typical of you isn't it, all sighing and silences. Don't think I haven't noticed them. You better watch it . . .'

'Watch what? What are you going to do?'

'I can do what I like, this is my band; one phone call and you're gone forever!' screamed Ollie.

'Gone? What do you mean gone? Are you threatening to do away with me, you know, kill me?! You heard that guys didn't you?' Hector said, talking to the camera crew. 'He wants me dead! Call the police! No, call my publicists!'

'No, not kill you!' Ollie yelled. 'I mean fire you!'

'Fire me?! That's worse!' screeched Hector.

'How is it worse than killing you?'

'Because it is! How are *you* going to *fire* me?'

'By firing you, that's how I'm going to fire you!' Ollie stood up. This was quickly escalating into a blazing row.

The camera operator looked at Charlie James, who mouthed 'keep rolling' back at him. Charlie knew this was gold. A blazing row would be great TV viewing.

'FIRE ME!? You can't fire me; it's not *your* band!' Hector said, getting to his feet. 'Maybe I'll fire *you*!' he said, prodding a finger into Ollie's shoulder.

'Did you just . . . just . . . prod me?!' Ollie said, looking in horror at Hector's finger. 'You know I have issues with my personal space. You need spiritual permission to come into my personal space!'

'Spiritual permission?! You've lost it mate. You're lost in showbiz!'

'Me?' Ollie replied in horror. 'You can talk. I mean, you have to have a basket of fruit with you wherever you go! That's not normal!'

'Oh, here you go again, always with the fruit mockery.'

'Keep this up and you'll be off, out on your ear,' Ollie threatened.

'I told you, you can't do that; it's my band too!' Hector screamed back.

'NO, IT'S MINE!' Ollie bellowed.

'IT'S MY KEYBOARD!'

'IT'S MY RECORDING EQUIPMENT!'

'MY LYRICS!'

'MY . . . CAT!' Ollie yelled at the top of his voice.

'What?! Oh, you really want to go there, do you?' Hector snapped.

'Boys! Boys!' Charlie intervened. 'I'm sure your fans don't want to see you arguing like this. But as you mention Nigel, why don't you both, in your own words, tell me how it started?'

Ollie and Hector looked at each other, and then burst into laughter. 'Oh, we're just messing, Charlie. We're really mates again,' Ollie chuckled. 'We don't fight any more. Sorry that was mean.'

'You should have seen your face, Charlie!' Hector laughed. 'You looked like a scared pumpkin. Anyway, yes, the cat . . .'

And so Ollie and Hector told Charlie everything: how they became accidental rock stars, how they had the world at their feet, and how they almost lost it all, including each other. How Big Records had fired them, and how Nigel had gone on to be the world's biggest selling act of all time. Apparently, all it took was some catnip on the keys and Nigel would play away for hours and hours. And as for Ollie and Hector . . .?

'Welcome back to *Where Are They Now?* with me, the ever-youthful Charlie James. Please do not adjust your set; my skin really is this orange. Let's talk about the reunion gig.'

'Well, it was a no-brainer really. I mean, yes, we weren't the true creators of *Cat Attack*, but as soon as Doris fired us it felt like we had been given a new lease of life. People wanted to hear our music, maybe not as many people but still, the offers started to come in, from people who were genuinely interested in our sound and our story,' Ollie said.

'We've got Ollie's Mum managing us now. Ollie's Dad's on security,' Hector added.

'It allows him to use a power hose on people for a living now. He's never been happier,' Ollie confirmed.

'But the best thing about it is we get to perform our own music. We still get requests from people asking us to play *Cat Attack*, but we say no,' Hector said, nodding.

'Yeah, it's not about the past, it's about the future, making new music—plus we're not allowed to play *Cat Attack* as Big Records have copyright and have threatened to take us to court. Is it the same as it was? No. The audience may be smaller, but it's *our* audience and it feels so much better.'

'Ollie, Hector . . .' Hannah called out, poking her head through the door. 'It's show time!'

'Band hug!' Hector said.

'Stay away from me Hector or I'll pull off your ears,' Hannah snarled.

'Fair doos.' Hector shrugged.

'Hannah, can I ask you, how does it feel to be back in the band along with your mum?' Charlie said, pushing a mic in her face.

'It feels good. It's a bit of a family business now,' Hannah said, smiling.

'Come on!' Mum said, peering round the door and twirling her drumsticks about.

'Got to go, Charlie!' Ollie said.

'Tell me guys, one last thing, are you nervous?' Charlie asked.

'It's been a big build up to this, our reunion gig, but there is no better feeling in the world. Finally, I can go out on stage and be myself,' Ollie said before taking a big breath and heading out onto stage.

'HELLO BUDLEIGH SALTERTON RETIREMENT HOME! IT'S NEARLY TIME FOR BINGO, BUT UNTIL THEN CAN I ASK YOU A QUESTION — ARE YOU READY TO ROCK?!'

NIGEL SIGNS MULTI-MILLION POUND DEAL!

N
CA

NIGEL SELLS OUT WORLD TOUR

NIGEL & LADY GA
ENGAGMENT

ALSO BY
Tom McLaughlin

TOM McLaughlin

YOU'VE BEEN WERE-WOLFED

THE APP THAT BITES BACK!

ABOUT THE AUTHOR

Before becoming a writer and illustrator, Tom spent nine years working as political cartoonist for *The Western Morning News* thinking up silly jokes about even sillier politicians. Then, in 2004 Tom took the plunge into illustrating and writing his own books. Since then he has written and illustrated fiction and picture books as well as working on animated TV shows for Disney and Cartoon Network.

Tom lives in Devon and his hobbies include drinking tea, looking out of the window, and biscuits. His hates include spiders, and running out of tea and biscuits.

READY FOR MORE GREAT STORIES? TRY ONE OF THESE . . .

ACTION STAN

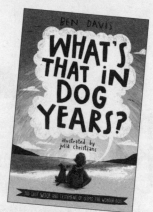

WHAT'S THAT IN DOG YEARS

COSMIC ATLAS

THE DEMON HEADMASTER
MORTAL DANGER